REVILE

OTHER BOOKS IN THE DISSENTER SAGA UNIVERSE
BY JOSEPHINE LAMONT

Revile: A Dissenter Saga Novel*

Dissent

Resist

Rise

*Prequel novel written in The Dissenter Saga universe. It can be read separately as a standalone, or enjoyed as part of the larger series. It does not need to be read in order to enjoy the other novels in The Dissenter Saga world.

REVILE

Josephine Lamont

Charter House Press

This book is a work of fiction. Names, characters, places, and incidents are the product of the author's imagination or are used fictitiously. Any resemblance to actual events, locales, or persons, living or dead, is coincidental.

Copyright © 2024 by Josephine Lamont. All rights reserved, including the right to reproduce, distribute, or transmit in any form or by any means. No part of this publication may be reproduced, distributed, or transmitted in any form or by any means, including photocopying, recording, or other electronic or mechanical methods, without the prior written permission of the publisher, except as permitted by U.S. copyright law. For permission requests, contact Josephine Lamont at jlamontbooks.com.

Edited by Tayler Bailey McLendon

Cover Design by 100Covers

ISBN 979-8-9913900-0-2 (Trade Paperback)

ISBN 979-8-3302-9649-1 (Hardback)

First edition October 2024

To my sisters. I love you.

Author Warning: *Revile* is a military-style fantasy book set in a brutal dystopian future. This book depicts issues of war, murder, death, intense violence (including gun violence), emotional and physical abuse, blood, electrocutions, graphic language, sexual intimacy depicted on the page, and incarceration. It is my hope that these elements have been handled sensitively, but if these issues could be considered triggering to you, please take note.

1: I Hate This, and That, and Definitely YOU

"June, can you tell me why the Western and Southern regions opted to secede from the United Factions of America?"

My head whipped forward, catching sight of my professor as she paced the front of the classroom. *Crap...* I racked my brain for the answer. Not the real answer, but the *right* one. The one that would keep me alive and my identity a secret.

"Miss Huang?"

"Looks like she failed to do the reading, Professor Watkins."

I snapped my head around and glared at Tim Harris with his stupid beady gray eyes and his stupid blond hair. He snickered, tapping Javier on the shoulder.

I swear to god, one day I'm going to stab that jack—

"*Miss Huang*," Professor Watkins snapped at me.

I faced forward again, trying to ignore the two jerks three rows behind me. "Yes, Professor?" She sounded so exasperated with me, and I couldn't blame her. Watkins had always been patient with me. But it was hard to regurgitate one history when you were taught a completely different set of events for your entire life.

She shook her head. "This will be on the Initiate Exam. I'd hate to see your application for graduation denied simply because you're not doing your homework."

"*Some*body's not graduating," Tim drawled once more from the back row. "District 3, here comes Junie."

"Es demasiado inteligente para estar en Distrito Tres," another voice sang from the back.

I gritted my teeth. If there was one person I hated more than Tim, it was Javier.

"Whatcha say, man? Whatcha say?" Freakin' Harris sounded damn right giddy. "Please tell me you called her Subclass Trash?"

I swiveled my head around.

Javier tucked his chin, glancing at me under hooded eyes. The stupid jerk was gorgeous with his glossy lengths of straight black hair and brown eyes so dark they actually looked like obsidian. Our coloring was similar, but where my skin looked like fine white china, his skin was tanned, deliciously kissed by the sun. He was the epitome of tall, dark, and ruggedly handsome. But he was full of himself, thinking that saying god only knows what in Spanish would cause any girl to drop to their knees. And the worst part was…he was freaking *right*! I absolutely hated it.

"Something like that," he confirmed, never taking his gaze off me. He was smoldering. How the hell did he make jackassery look so damn good? And how was it that guys could *smolder*? *I* wanted to *smolder*. But whenever I tried, I just looked like an idiot.

"Speak *English*," I snapped back at him. "At least have the guts to insult me in a language I understand."

I watched him lean forward over his desk with a sexy arched brow. "Acculturate yourself, mi vida. Then see if you have the courage to face me."

I chewed on my cheek, seething. *I hate de la Puentes.*

Watkins clapped her hands, bringing the attention back to her. "Enough, Mr. de la Puente. And please, speak in English."

I smirked. *Thank you, Professor.*

"Miss Huang," Watkins faced me again. "Do you know the answer or not?"

I inhaled deeply, trying to calm my temper. It was not my best quality. I looked at my teacher. *The West and South* didn't *secede from the UFA. Raúl murdered their ruling families in cold blood after earning their trust, and then separated from the rest of the United Factions to form Telvia.* That was the *real* answer.

I cleared my throat. "The West and South seceded after the third civil war, when the people rose against their monarchical presidents because they desired a true democracy and the power of choice. At the time, President de la Puente was General of the West. He took control of the Western faction and promised the people a free election."

Professor Watkins smiled. "Very good, Miss Huang." Her eyes finally left mine and scanned the room. "And why did the United States become the United Factions of America to begin with?"

Sally raised her hand. She was one of the few people I actually tolerated around here. "The Great Drought, Professor. Because of climate change, erratic weather patterns emerged and led to a severe, sustained drought, food shortages, and natural weather disasters that devastated the nation."

"Excellent, Miss Miller. And how did climate change alter the future of the USA?"

Sally glanced my way, and I offered her an encouraging smile in return. These were all questions we needed to know for the Citizenship portion of our Initiate's Exam. In a week, we would all graduate as long as we passed the exam tomorrow.

Movement two rows up caught my attention as Chase raised his hand. He was arguably one of the most popular boys at the Telvian Academy, rivaled only by the de la Puente cousins—Javier and Jacob. Chase was the exact opposite of Javier in his appearance—blond, bright green eyes, angular features, and a jaw that looked like it could crack marble. More important than that, he was a good guy, and he was my friend.

"Mr. Beckham?"

"Due to the lack of natural resources caused by the weather, the states grew greedy with what resources they had. No one wanted to share. Fighting broke out, and the country experienced the second civil war, causing the USA's government to collapse."

"Well done, Mr. Beckham."

Chase smiled, clearly pleased with himself. I smirked. *Show off.* That was the only thing about Chase…he could be a peacock.

The bell rang. Professor Watkins pulled back the sleeve of her blouse, glanced at her mini-tab, and then smiled at the room. "Enough review for today. Please be here bright and early tomorrow. The exam starts promptly at eight."

Thank the stars. I couldn't have been more ready to leave. While everyone else was going out with friends, I had more important things to do. I grabbed my backpack, shoved my e-reader in it, and got out of there like a bat out of hell before Sally had a chance of asking me to study with her tonight.

The hallways were a mess of students, and there was a clamor of chatter, laughter, and locker doors banging. I reached mine and typed in my code. It beeped, flashing a little green light, and unlocked. In my opinion, lockers were pointless. No one had actual books anymore, especially in Telvia. Raúl had them all destroyed when he took power and proclaimed himself the president of the Western and Southern factions of the UFA. He curated which books were allowed, keeping just enough classic works to keep the people from suspecting censorship.

But he was censoring all right. He was censoring *big* time.

In fact, the whole freaking city was being censored from the rest of the world. Nobody realized that the rest of the continent was alive and thriving. I blew out a breath. It was the hardest thing knowing the truth and trying to pretend like you didn't know squat.

"Hey!"

I jumped. "Damn it, Sally, don't sneak up on me like that." This girl had no idea who she was dealing with. She was so freaking lucky I didn't stab her with my daggers. I had two—one attached to each thigh under my navy-blue uniform skirt. And they had names: Honor and Glory.

"I'm sorry. You just left class so fast, and I wanted to talk to you." Sally was a sweet, mousy thing. Small and petite, with auburn hair and blue-green eyes hidden behind round glasses. But she was always nervous and lacked confidence—a by-product of being from District 3. No one from District 3 had much of anything, *especially* confidence.

I shook my head, biting my tongue, and pulled out my gym clothes. It was my last class, and I absolutely hated gym. Not only did I have to leave my daggers behind, but I had to pretend like I couldn't hand every guy his own ass on a silver platter.

"About what?" I slammed my locker closed.

"About the party this weekend…the graduation party. Are you going?" She smiled brightly.

"*Harris's* party? Oh no," I said as I backed away from the locker. "You know Harris and I don't play nice."

She gripped my shoulder, skipping along beside me. "*Please*," she begged. "*He's* going to be there, and I really need you," she said, pouting her bottom lip.

I stuck my finger in my mouth and made an obnoxious gagging sound.

She glared. "Don't be that way. Jacob's really sweet."

I rolled my eyes at her. She wasn't wrong. For being the son of Telvia's president-turned-dictator, he wasn't bad. Full of himself, just like his cousin, and grossly flawed in his politics, but significantly better than some of the other District 1 snobs. That district was nothing more than a collection of society's elite—the Noble Class. Just a bunch of rotten, no-good wealthy politicians that kept Raúl in power.

Sally was from the Subclass, and I was assigned District 2 status when I entered Telvia undercover. Three districts. Three castes. And they all varied hugely in status and wealth. But everyone received the same education at the Academy. From five until eighteen, everyone attended the same brick-and-mortar building, getting the same brainwashing crap as everybody else.

A dying earth, destroyed by our own hands.

A conflicted nation tearing itself apart.

Civil war. Government collapse.

And the rise of an independent country—Telvia.

It wasn't *all* BS. In fact, all of it was true. The lie was how Raúl de la Puente was going to reintroduce democracy to the two factions he took by force.

That part was the lie.

Because once he tasted sweet power, he never let it go. And now, almost two decades later, half of the former UFA still believed that the world beyond their giant freaking wall was nothing but desert infested with marauders. Telvians believed the rest of the UFA had completely collapsed after the last war—The Loyal War.

Idiots.

But I shouldn't be so hard on them. For nearly twenty years, Telvians were taught that the rest of the world was gone. No one could go beyond the wall unless you had military clearance, and all media was scrutinized and controlled. Nothing got in and nothing got out. It was like living under a freaking dome. How people hadn't gotten fed up and taken up arms already, I didn't know.

"So will you go?"

I turned my attention back to Sally. "I don't know, Sal"—I dodged someone rushing down the hall—"I'm pretty busy."

She skipped in front of me and planted herself like a damn rock. Hands on her hips, Sally Miller stared me down. "Doing what, June? Tomorrow's the exam and then it's done. It's all over." She narrowed her eyes. "What could you possibly have to do?"

"Uh…" *Rebel stuff. You know, report to my commanding officer, be briefed on my mission, and then get the hell out of Telvia before I get caught.*

"Damn it," I muttered.

"Yes!" Sally hopped, clapping her hands.

Stepping around her, I hustled down the hall, already running late for freaking gym. "I didn't say I was going," I tossed over my shoulder.

"But you *have* to go!" She grabbed onto my arm again. "You know I can't go unless someone from a higher district takes me. *Please,* June. Pretty please…for me?"

There it was. I looked at Sally once again. She looked like she was about to cry, her hands up like she was praying to the universe.

I groaned. "God, Sally, I hate you so much," I groused.

"Does that mean you'll go?"

I wrinkled my nose. "I'll *think* about it," I said, hating that I was even *considering* going to Harris's damn party.

She threw her arms around me, hopping once more. "Thank you, thank you, thank you!"

"That wasn't a *yes*," I muttered, untangling myself from her arms. "Thank me once I agree because there's a huge chance I'll say no."

Freaking Telvians.

"I know you won't," she gushed. "See you after school!" Then she was gone.

I trilled my lips. Of all the damn things, it had to be Harris's party. I shivered. I *hated* Harris. The jerk deserved to have his eyes pecked out by a chicken.

I groaned again as I stepped out into the light of the afternoon sun. Everything was concrete and artificial turf around here, but at least the sun was real. I soaked it in as much as I could before I shoved open the double doors to the gymnasium only to be smacked by the smell of sweat and rubber. And when I looked across the massive indoor basketball court, blue rubber mats were all over the floor.

Dread filled every corner of my five-foot-seven frame. Not today. It was the last day of gym. Why the hell were we doing this *toda*y?

"Huang!" Coach Bill yelled across the room. "Get your ass in your gym clothes. Let's go!"

I closed my eyes, gritting my teeth. *Sparring*. Why the hell were we freaking sparring?

I hated sparring.

I hated gym.

I hated this stupid Academy.

I hated the caste system that kept good people like Sally stuck with less.

I hated Tim Harris.

I hated Telvia.

I hated all of it!

"Huang, did you hear me?" Coach shouted again. "Get ready and get on the damn mat."

My name's not Huang, I thought to myself.

I kicked ass and took names with two blades I was lethally trained to use. And one day, we were going to tear this Academy down brick by freaking brick, lie by fucking lie. One day soon, the Telvian people would be free, and the entire de la Puente family would pay for the crimes they committed against the United Factions of America.

My name is Liddy Le, and I am most definitely ready.

2: Cleanup on Mat 2

Sparring was an essential part of gym class because it allowed the Telvians to see if you would be any good for a career in military or enforcement. It was only in your last year at the Academy, and only done a few weeks before Initiation. They gave you very little instruction on what to do or how to do it.

And why would they? The last thing a dictator wants is his citizens to be armed or trained for combat, right? Such things would only arm the people to take back control.

But graduation was this Saturday, and the Initiation Ceremony would determine our future caste, careers, and the rest of our lives. In Telvia, everything you did at the Academy from age five to eighteen was an assessment. One big, long-ass test for the Telvian Council to determine your strengths and weaknesses. They took all that info and determined where *they* thought you belonged.

The wealthy, powerful, and strong were in the Noble Class—District 1.

Those too smart for their own good were typically in the Middle Class—District 2. Intelligent people were an asset to the Telvian government but could be hard to manipulate. District 2 gave them just enough status to keep them happy without the same power and control as the Nobles.

Those deemed as feeble and a drain on society were in the Subclass—District 3. But it also housed the troublemakers—those individuals considered problematic to the Telvian Council. They lived on the fringes of society, receiving less than everyone else, and barely survived each year.

Raúl's philosophy was to keep those who supported his reign and ideals happy and in a position of power. Those who could overthrow him needed to be kept weak and in line. And everyone else sat in the middle.

Wanted to move up? You had thirteen years to prove you deserved to be promoted to a higher class while at the Academy. That was it. That was your shot. After that, your life was set in stone, and you were stuck. Chances of being promoted following the Academy were rare, and you were far more likely to be demoted into a lower caste. And absolutely no one wanted to be dropped a class.

I tugged on my gym shorts, trying to cover more of my thighs as I walked onto the court toward the four blue mats set up like a game of four square in the middle of the gym. Coach stood in the middle where all four corners met. A quick glance at the bleachers showed me that several members of the Initiate Committee were here.

Ah...I get it now. This was a final assessment before graduation. One last look at who had enough brutality in them to be assigned a career in Telvian Enforcement or the REG—Rebel Enforcement Group. *Figures...I should have known better.*

"Mat 1, Huang." Coach pointed to the upper righthand corner.

Blowing out a breath, I started walking to the mat, watching as Chase threw down some redhead on Mat 4. The coach blew his whistle and ordered him off the mat.

Chase offered the redhead a hand, pulled him up to his feet, and then stepped off the mat before walking my way. His bright green eyes caught mine, and I couldn't help but smirk as he leaned down to whisper something to me. Shoulder to shoulder, I looked at him.

"Is your pride stuck in *show-off* mode, *Beckham?*"

His eyes gleamed. "There's no harm in showing them what I can do," he answered with a smile.

I gave him an exaggerated eye roll. "I don't know why I expected anything less."

He leaned in close, lips coming to my ear. "It's the last day. No harm in showing them what *you've* got, either."

I pulled back just enough to see that stupid, charming face of his. I liked Chase. But not like *that*. We were just friends. And even if I *did* like him like that, it was going to be a *hard pass* on his part. Because he had his eyes set on one girl and one girl only. And that girl sure as hell wasn't me.

I smirked at him. "Yeah, we'll see."

"Huang!" the coach yelled again. "Mat *1!*"

I groaned as Chase patted me on the back. "Go get 'em, *June.*"

I turned my attention back to the mats and kept walking. A nervous girl with curly black hair was waiting for me on Mat 1. I pulled my long, sleek, raven-black hair into a ponytail, and then stepped onto the blue rubber, feeling it give under the weight of my body. The whistle blew, and it took me all of five minutes before she tapped out.

I didn't even try.

It was kind of sad. I looked at the bleachers and watched as the Initiate Committee took several notes. Unless the girl was brilliant or wealthy AF, she was heading straight for District 3 if she wasn't already. I advanced onto Mat 2.

My next opponent was a boy with a buzz cut and gangly frame. Licking my lips, I stepped back onto the mat. He was going to be more of a challenge, hopefully. The whistle blew, and I crouched down, ready to move. The boy charged me, but he was sloppy and off balance. Way too low and yet, somehow, not low enough. I evaded him easily, shifting left. He spun around, hands out like he was going to grapple with a tiger or something, leaving his face and sides totally exposed.

Idiot. Drop your damn arms.

He charged me again. I swept to the right this time, dodging him once more. But this time, as he passed me, I shot out my left arm in a karate-chop motion, smacking him hard in the kidney. He groaned, and I winced for him. I knew that had to hurt. I just hoped I didn't hit him hard enough for him to pee blood tonight.

I spun around and watched as he arched his back, one hand cupping the spot where I hit him. I grimaced. *Poor guy.*

"Fucking bitch," he muttered.

Never mind. I no longer felt sympathy for him. I crouched back into my fighting stance. "This *bitch* is ready to deliver again whenever you're done crying."

He glared at me, and then charged. Had he learned nothing?

I let him close the gap, and he was just as uncoordinated as before. But instead of dodging, I dropped, swung out a leg, and sent him crashing to the ground. Before he moved, I pounced like a jungle cat and grabbed his arm, twisted it behind his back, and applied enough pressure to incapacitate him.

"How does that feel?" I asked, increasing the pressure by just a hair.

"Ow!" he yelled, his face smothered in the rubber mat. "I'm done!" He tapped the mat twice with his free hand, and I let him go, backing away quickly.

The whistle blew, and the coach yelled out, "Mat 3, Huang!"

I split my hair into two and pulled, tightening my ponytail as I stepped off the mat. The boy grumbled as he got up, muttering obscenities under his breath as he called me several more unpleasant names. I flipped him off.

Jackass.

I twisted my head, cracking my neck as I stepped onto Mat 3. The boy across from me was facing away, watching whatever was happening on Mat 4. All I saw was the back of his blond head until he finally turned around. Gray eyes met mine, and a sneer that would have curdled milk.

"Shit," I muttered under my breath.

Tim Harris laughed. "Oh, today is my lucky fucking day! I would have given anything to spar with you, Huang."

I narrowed my eyes at him as I stepped across the mat. "Didn't think you'd be so desperate to have your ass handed to you, Harris. Especially in front of the Committee."

He laughed…like Santa Claus. Grabbed his abs like it was a bowl full of damn jelly. But Harris was anything but jelly. The guy was built like an ox with broad, bulky shoulders and a neck so thick it looked like a damn tree trunk.

I slowly dropped into my fighting stance.

Tim shook his head as he crouched. "It's like an early graduation present," he said with a cocky grin. "I'm going to do you a solid, Huang. I'm going to drop kick your ass into District 3 and save you the embarrassing walk of shame as my personal graduation present to you. Because I'm a nice guy like that."

Now I knew why Chase told me there was no harm in showing off—he knew exactly who was waiting for me on the mat. I smiled, feeling adrenaline and pure elation pumping through my veins. I was going to give Harris a taste of his own medicine.

I'm going to kick your ass so hard, you're going to shit sideways. I snickered at my thought. "Bring it on, Harris. Let's show the Committee your true colors."

The whistle blew, and it was on.

3: Kicking Ass and Taking Names

I toyed with him. Harris was big and strong, but he was slow, and he gave every move away with a little twitch in the arm or leg he planned to use next.

So. Freaking. Obvious.

I easily dodged him, and then…

SMACK.

Twirled to the right…

PUNCH.

Spun left…

KICK.

He huffed. He groaned. He coughed. He growled.

But no matter how much he came at me, I evaded him easily. It was kind of fun, actually, and I was tiring him out. All of his lumbering punches took a lot of energy, and he was growing fatigued.

"Enough, Huang," he growled at me as I slipped past him again. I spun around and kicked him in the butt, sending him falling forward onto his face.

The entire gym broke out laughing. And not just little titters. They were *rolling*. Even the Committee was chuckling in the stands. They were trying to hide it, but they were doing a piss-poor job of it.

I watched Harris as he climbed to his feet, beet red and looking like he was about to explode.

"I thought you were going to send me flying to District 3, Harris?" I held my hands out, palms up. "What happened? I was looking forward to the flight." The vein in his left temple bulged, and I swore I could see steam blowing out his ears. I stood up straight, placing a thoughtfully pointed finger on my chin. "Now, Tim, be careful with your blood pressure. I wouldn't want people to think the only reason I kicked your sorry, Noble butt was because you had a heart attack on the mat."

The dude screamed. He clenched both fists and gave out a primal, guttural yell that truly looked like a gorilla getting ready for a throw down. *Oops.* I might have poked his pride just a little too hard.

As if to confirm, he lunged at me. But for once, he didn't have that stupid twitch, and I didn't know which arm he was coming at me with. I guessed and moved left.

Missed me again.

Except he didn't.

As I spun past him, he whipped out and grabbed my ponytail, wrapping it around his fist with one fluid roll of his wrist, and *yanked*. I fell backwards onto the mat, landing hard on my back. Instinct and training took over, and I let out a big kiai, expelling all the air from my lungs to keep from having the wind knocked out of me. And then I was being dragged.

My hands shot to my scalp, gripping the base of my ponytail as Harris pulled me along the mat by my hair.

The whistle blew. "Illegal move, Harris!" It was the coach. He blew his whistle again, but Harris gave me one more good, hard yank by the hair, before letting go.

"You son of a—*oof!*" Tim kicked me right in the stomach.

"Tap out, Huang," Coach yelled from the side of the mat.

Like *hell* I was going to tap out. I snapped my attention back to Tim as he swung his leg forward to kick me again. But I was ready this time. I caught his foot and twisted it so fast he didn't have time to react. He came crashing down like a freaking tree, face into the mat. I rolled onto my back and kicked up, snapping onto the balls of my feet from the ground. Several people in the crowd cheered in awe as I leapt onto Harris, grabbed his arm and twisted it behind his back in an elegant, unnatural looking S.

He squealed as I applied pressure. "Tap out, Harris," I said through gritted teeth. *What I* should *do is break your freaking arm.* Harris was a bully, and everyone knew it. But his daddy was the general of the REG, so he never got the punishment he deserved. I couldn't count the times I saw him pick on the little kids during lunch or demeaning those from lower districts. He was the guy that would have grown up torturing dogs and cats if Telvians were permitted pets. He was a serious menace. A freaking sociopath in the making.

"Go to hell, Huang," he spat on the mat.

"Now, Tim…" I twisted a little harder, listening to him inhale sharply. "That's not very nice. Tap. The fuck. Out. Or I swear to god, I'll break your wrist."

He growled, but there was literally nothing he could do. I had him. With a yell half muffled by the mat, Tim tapped his free hand twice just as the school bell rang.

I let him go and backed away fast, making sure I stayed clear of both his hands as I stepped off the mat. He came to his feet, and the look on his face screamed only one word as his storm gray eyes collided with mine.

Murder.

They screamed that if he was ever given the opportunity, he was going to flat out *murder* me.

He pointed at me, but he didn't dare come closer. "This isn't over, Huang. I swear you're going to regret messing with me." Then he turned and walked back toward the lockers.

"I think you've made an enemy," a smooth, accented voice whispered in my ear.

I spun around, instinct taking over as I swung my right fist through the air, aiming to clock whoever the heck it was, right in the temple. But with a swift lift of his left arm, he blocked me just as he swiped out with his right hand and snagged my wrist, yanking me close to his beautiful face.

Black waves of hair.

Sinful onyx eyes.

Lips twisted in a devilish smirk.

Freaking Javier de la Puente.

"Let. Go." I pushed the words out through my clenched jaw. I was so focused on Tim, I let this jerk right into my personal space.

"Eres violenta," he whispered, his face way too close to mine.

I narrowed my gaze at him. "What did you say to me?"

He tipped his head to the side. "I said you're violent."

I yanked my wrist, but his grip only tightened. Inhaling deeply, I tried to calm my temper. I wasn't scared. Not even a bit. I could take Javier down just as easily as the gangly boy on Mat 2, no doubt. But he was a de la Puente, and we weren't sparring. School was officially over, and taking down the Telvian president's nephew was the fastest way to blow my cover and have my ass shipped off to a reeducation camp. Then I would never see the light of day again.

"You know, it's rude to speak about people in a language they don't understand. I told you already, if you're going to insult me, have the guts to say it in English."

He finally loosened his grip, and I yanked my wrist free. But I didn't back down. Oh, hell no. I just dropped my wrist and dug my nails into the flesh of my palms.

"Maybe it wasn't an insult." He flashed me a grin. "Maybe it was a compliment."

I squeaked, taken aback. Javier chuckled.

Keep it together, Lin. Keep it together. I took a deep breath. I wanted nothing more than to tell him where to go and how to get there, but he was off limits. I exhaled and leaned a hair forward, our noses millimeters from grazing each other. His eyes flickered, and the dark abyss of them shifted to my mouth.

Good. He can read my lips. "You're. Not. Worth it," I whispered slowly. And I meant it. There was only one de la Puente worth anything in this stupid city, and she wasn't my responsibility.

I stepped back away from him, keeping my narrowed gaze on his.

He held his head high. "Maybe one day, mi vida, you'll find me worthy of you." He smiled. The jerk actually smiled at me.

"Not likely." I spun around and marched back to the locker room, leaving him in the dust.

4: Little Sis

"Home" was really my undercover dwelling in District 2. And my single mother, May Huang, was completely unrelated to me. Her last name, however, *was* Huang, and she used to be married. May and Andrew were both Dissenters—former Telvians turned rebels, fed up with Raúl and the Telvian Council. She was widowed after her husband died a year ago in an accident that killed him and their seventeen-year-old daughter, June—who bore an uncanny resemblance to me. Thus, my ability to slip in and take Junie's place with no one being the wiser.

Taking over June's life had been…interesting.

Despite outer appearances, it turns out *Junie* and I shared little in common. Where she was meek and shy, I tended to be loud and boisterous. Where she was organized and contained, I was…well, I was sort of all over the place.

Although May and Andrew were Dissenters, June was not. Her parents didn't want to risk her making a mistake—speaking ill of the Telvian government or the de la Puente family, or accidentally giving away her affiliation with a rebel group—and have her taken to a reeducation camp.

Nobody wanted to go to a reeducation camp. Serious bad news there.

So they raised her to be a good Telvian citizen despite being Dissenters themselves.

This made things tricky for me. Not only did I have to pretend to be *her*, but I had to act *nothing* like myself. I wasn't cut out for acting. It was never my thing. And yet, here I was…rounding a year of undercover work, pretending to be someone I wasn't. And holy baby monkeys everywhere, it was tough.

A year of nourishment pills and no cheeseburgers.

A year of dealing with Telvians and their BS caste system.

A year of freaking Tim Harris and his stupidity and bullying.

A whole. Freaking. Year of damn Javier de la Puente and his incessant pestering that was driving me insane.

I mean, don't get me wrong, Harris deserved to have an apple shoved in his mouth, be impaled on a stick, slathered in BBQ sauce, and cooked over an open fire for cannibals. But at least the man had the freaking guts to insult you to your face. To make sure you knew what he was saying and not make conflicting gestures in the process. I respected that. Made the relationship crystal clear, and there was nothing better than having clear, straight lines in a daily life of confusing blurred edges between reality and fiction.

But Mr. Spanish Mambo King lacked the guts to insult me in English. What a coward. He was no better than Harris, incessantly bothering me but hiding behind melodic foreign insults instead of just freaking owning it like a man. In that regard, I preferred Tim. I knew how to deal with guys like Tim. Tim I could handle.

But Javier…that guy…that guy was going to make me pull my hair out. That guy made me want to shove my foot so high up his pompous ass that he tasted shoe leather.

But he was off limits. And god didn't that drive me nuts.

Every day was an effort, constantly checking myself to make sure I wasn't going to give myself away somehow. But it got easier. Little by little, Junie became me…or rather, I became Junie. I softened myself some, and people got used to June's new attitude, chalking it up to trauma following the accident. And I slipped into a routine that worked…mostly.

People like Sally and Chase made it easier. They gave me a tribe while I managed the ridiculousness that was the Academy. And May, she took me in and cared for me just like I really was her daughter. It made things easier to have someone like May, someone who was steady and calming and level-headed, around.

But May wasn't my mom. Telvia wasn't my home. And I *missed* home.

My actual home was beyond Telvia's walls in a region known as the North, thus making me a Northerner. And when I turned sixteen, I was permitted to enlist in the army, which paid incredibly well, allowing me to send money home to support my family. My real parents were farmers, and they were freaking bunnies. I was the oldest of seven. And why they thought that having more kids after the first three was beyond me. Frankly, I didn't care either. I loved my family, and that was all that mattered.

"Liddy? Is that you?"

"Yeah, it's me," I said, closing the front door behind me. The Huang house was pleasant enough, with a little entryway and a curved staircase that led upstairs. All the District 1 families lived in luxury, but District 2 was a little dicier, and District 3…well, that was the slums. But most of us who were undercover were placed in District 2 or below. It was just too hard to get someone placed in District 1. The only way to do it was with a long undercover operation, where someone worked their way up at the Academy. It was a colossal pain in the butt. Lots of risk and little reward.

May stepped in from the living room. "How did it go?" She was a plain-looking woman, but sweet as could be.

"Fine, I guess. I had sparring assessments today."

"And?"

"I creamed Tim Harris."

May scoffed, giving me a disappointed look. "Liddy, you know better."

I lifted a hand, quieting her. "Spare me the lecture, May—"

"You're going to get yourself caught," she spoke over me. "And not just yourself, but *me*, too."

I winced. She was right. One thing was risking myself. Another thing was risking somebody else's cover too. "Yeah, you're right. I'm sorry." I faced her. Watched as she pressed her lips into a thin line.

Her eyes flickered for a moment, and then she nodded. "Thank you."

I blew out a breath. We had an understanding. No unnecessary risks. An uncomfortable minute ticked by. Then, "Any orders?"

She shook her head. "No, but I'm sure they'll assign you something as soon as they know your new position."

I nodded. Right now, it was hard for me to do much during the day. But after the Initiation Ceremony, I'd be assigned a District, a career, and told where I would live. Everything was decided for you.

Determined.

Controlled.

There was no choice. There was no freedom. There were no options.

Think the way they tell you. Behave the way they say. Do as you're freaking told.

But I wasn't a Telvian.

"I'm going to call home," I informed her. Without waiting, I raced up the stairs and into my room. Deep in my dresser, I had my unregulated Holo Box. It was a little black device that projected the person you were speaking to in a 3D rendering right before your eyes. The image was always clear, though the projection system gave off a bluish hue, distorting the colors slightly.

I placed the device at the foot of my bed and climbed up, crossing my legs on the mattress. With a few taps, I inputted Edith's contact info and waited, watching a little light blink yellow, letting me know it was trying to reach her. After a moment, it switched to green. A flash of blue light rose from the box, and an image of a girl who looked like a younger replica of me formed before my eyes.

Edith Le was two years younger, with the same sleek, black hair, almond-shaped brown eyes, and porcelain skin as me. We looked like dolls, with smooth delicate features. If you didn't know any better, you'd swear we were breakable.

We were anything but.

"Liddy!" Edith squealed. "How have you been? I was wondering when you'd call again."

I smiled. "Hey, little sis. I'm good, just busy, you know? How are Mom and Dad?"

She snorted. "Tending the crops. Harvest is in a few months. Are you going to be home to help?"

I shook my head. "I haven't been told my assignment yet. But I hope I'll be able to go home soon. I miss you all so much." A thought popped into my head. "Hey, did you guys get the money I sent home?"

Edith nodded. "Yeah, Mom got it the other day."

"Was it enough? Is it going to cover the cost?"

She smiled. "Yeah, it did. They're going to schedule her surgery for next month."

I sighed, closing my eyes and feeling a swell of relief. Our youngest sister needed to have her tonsils removed. Not a big deal, but Mom and Dad didn't have the money to cover the surgery. What I got paid for being in the military helped support my family, but because I was also undercover in Telvia, I got hazard pay—a supplemental income for doing dangerous work. I was hoping my last check would cover the cost of her surgery, and it looked like it was going to be just enough.

"You know, Lin, I turn sixteen in a few months—"

I cut her off. "Don't even think about it. I've got this. Help them on the farm. There's no need to enlist when I have it covered."

She scoffed. "And why should *you* have all the fun?"

I glared. "It's not *fun*, it's dangerous. Mom and Dad don't need to be worried about both of us."

She rolled her eyes so hard I thought her eyeballs were going to get stuck staring at the back of her head. "I'm enlisting."

"No, you're not, Edith."

She crossed her arms. "Just because you're older doesn't mean you can boss me around. Besides, I got a good look at the guys who were enlisting yesterday and—holy shit—they were sexy as *hell*!"

I shook my head. "Oh brother," I groaned.

Her tone switched like a light being turned on. "Please tell me you found yourself a hottie?" she purred.

I started laughing. Leave it to flipping Edith. "Even if I did, I'm in Telvia, sis. No nothing with anybody."

"Wait, what? Are you serious?"

I cocked a brow, nodding slowly. "Super serious."

Her eyes looked like dinner plates. "*Nothing*? Like absolutely *nothing*?"

"Nothing." I confirmed. "If you get caught just kissing someone without a Match Permit, you're in deep shit."

Her jaw hit the floor. "No wonder why they give you hazard pay. Celibacy is a severe condition, resulting in the shriveling up of your lady bits—"

I started laughing. Her face looked dead serious as she continued saying the most ridiculous stuff.

"I hear that the guy's junk falls off from dehydration and lack of stimulation—"

"Oh my god, *stop!*" I ordered as I folded my arms over my stomach and kept laughing. I knew she was joking, but I had a sneaking suspicion some part of her was a hundred percent serious. If it weren't because Mom and Dad were like freaking bunnies themselves, I'd seriously question where her sexual appetite came from.

She started giggling, her hologram flickering for a moment. "Well, if you're not allowed to play, then I hope they're all pug ugly."

I scrunched my brows. "*Hey,*" I drawled. "Pugs are super cute!"

"Like hell they are. They're all wrinkly and chubby."

"And that makes them adorable."

"It makes them *pugly*."

"*You're* pugly."

"I'm freaking gorgeous," she asserted. "And you know it, so don't even try contradicting me."

I smiled. I adored my little sister. We were best friends. Always had been, and always would be.

A warning flashed on my Holo Box, letting me know I had to cut the transmission or it risked being caught by the REG. Sending transmissions in and out of Telvia was always risky. But if you kept them short enough, you could avoid it being detected.

"I gotta go, lil' sis."

"One day, you're going to have to stop calling me that. I'm not little anymore."

"And one day when you *actually* mature, I'll consider it," I said with a smile.

"You'll call me again soon?"

"I'll try." My heart squeezed. "Give everyone my love?"

"You got it. I love you, Lin."

"I love you, too. Bye, Edith."

"Bye."

The sinking feeling in my stomach grew as I watched her hologram disappear. I hated hanging up. Because every time I hung up, I couldn't help but wonder if it would be the last time I said goodbye. And just like every other time before, I feared it was. But it sat heavier on me tonight. It felt like a brick of lead smothering my heart. The only thing I could guess was that intuition was a real thing, screaming a warning that I would never see Edith again.

The worst part was…it was right.

5: The Initiate's Exam

Why has Telvia adopted nourishment pills as its primary source of nutrition for its people?

I was on question 153 out of 200 on the Initiate Exam. Even after the extensive combat training I'd received since joining the military, exams like this had a way of wearing me out. I ran my hand through my hair as I thought about the question.

The *real* answer? The more people depended on their government for resources, the more control the government had over them. A cursory look at any other government fallen prey to a crazy dictator proved that to be true over and over again.

But that wasn't even an option among the multiple-choice answers. I read them through, lingering on the last option.

Nourishment pills allow the Telvian government to create the perfect nutrition for each individual and eliminate greenhouse gas emissions caused by raising livestock by almost 18%.

I selected that option and moved on to the next question.

True or False: Since its invention, nourishment pills have eliminated food waste by 99%.

That was actually true. The downside was there was absolutely nothing to eat or drink in Telvia except for the stupid pills and water. God, I hated being undercover here. I missed cheeseburgers and fries. My mouth watered just at the thought of it. I blew out a breath and moved on to the next question.

What Telvian technology replaced all handheld communication devices (including cell phones) and all other smartwatches?

Easy...way too freaking easy. The mini-tab, *duh*. I glanced at the sleek black watch on my wrist. This was a Telvian one. My *real* tab—the one I brought from home when I was assigned to assist in the Dissenter rebellion—I hid in my bra.

True or False: Trackers are inserted into the forearm of each Telvian citizen at birth to help maintain the security of all individuals.

I schooled my face to keep from scoffing at the screen. This was, unfortunately, true. Everyone was implanted with a tracker, but not for security. For control. So the Council could monitor everybody's movements. Not only that, but you couldn't go two city blocks without having your retinas scanned by Telvian Enforcement in some areas. The rebel movement was growing, and Raúl knew it. He was getting nervous, and as a result, he was cracking down harder on the people.

I selected *true* and moved on to the next question.

It took me almost another hour to get through the last part of the exam, but I made it through, sighing with relief as I clicked *submit*. The screen prompted me to wait as it calculated my score for a few seconds, and then the screen changed.

Congratulations, Initiate. You have passed. Turn in your device and follow instructions provided by your proctor.

I closed my eyes and smiled. *Thank god. I never want to do that again.* And thankfully, after today, I never would. I stood up and walked to the front of the room, handing Professor Watkins my tablet. She eyed me with pursed lips, glanced at my screen, and then smiled.

"Well done, Miss Huang."

"Thanks, Professor," I whispered back, smiling like an idiot. I walked back to my desk and rested my head. Now I just had to wait.

***

The bell rang, and I leapt out of my seat and practically ran out of the room to my locker. Like every respectable student, I hated school. And like every senior, I couldn't wait to graduate on Saturday. It was just three days away, and the Initiation Ceremony would introduce all graduates to the community. And after that, I would finally get my orders from the Dissenters. I could complete whatever mission they had for me and finally go home.

Bing!

My Telvian tab sang on my wrist, telling me I had a message. I tapped the screen.

GRADUATION PARTY AT THE HARRIS HOUSE!
TIME: SATURDAY NIGHT @ 6:00 P.M.
MIDDLE AND NOBLE CLASS GRADUATES ONLY
NO SUBCLASS ALLOWED—NO EXCEPTIONS!

I glared at the screen. Tim was such an ass to exclude Subclass graduates. But I guess it wasn't just him. Everyone in District 1 thought their shit didn't stink, the jerks. I repressed a frustrated groan and just flicked the message away. Poor Sally was going to be heartbroken. Everyone knew Harris was throwing a party, and she wanted to go to this damn thing so bad. But the chances of her being promoted from District 3 into 2 or 1 were highly unlikely.

She was going to be discriminated against and excluded from the party no matter who she showed up with.

Freaking Tim. I hated him. I was glad I made him look like an idiot in front of the Committee. Maybe he'd be demoted to District 2.

Highly unlikely, the little voice in my head said.

But that doesn't mean I can't fantasize about it, I argued back with myself. That was a regular thing for me. My conscience had a mind of its own, sometimes.

I liked to think of it as my *women's intuition*, or maybe like a little devil on my shoulder. Whatever it was, I argued with it often.

I double checked that I didn't need anything from my locker and then slammed it closed. Huh…Sally wasn't here. Normally, she was buzzing by my locker like a fly, yapping my ear off about how dreamy she thought Jacob was. The fact that she wasn't here right now told me she was probably sobbing some place about this stupid invite.

I sighed. I should look for her…try to comfort her or something. Convince her that the party would be stupid anyway. I walked down the hall, keeping my eyes open for her coppery auburn hair. When I didn't see her among the students, I double checked the bathrooms, then raced to the gym to see if I would find her in the locker room there.

I struck out. I texted her several times, but she never responded either.

Where the hell was Sally?

A little tangle of angst started brewing in the pit of my stomach. Something wasn't right. Something was very, very wrong. I could feel it.

The school was clearing out, with most of the students already gone. All I could think was that Sally walked home, but we normally walked together until we got to the border between my district and the Subclass neighborhoods. Would she really walk home without me?

A part of me thought I should just drop it and go home, but a different part screamed in warning.

Find her, my intuition urged. *Find her, now!*

I listened. If there was one thing I had learned about myself through my two years of military and special ops training, it was to follow that little voice. My intuition was strong, and ninety-nine percent of the time, it was eerily right.

I left the school and started walking the route we always took home. Cameron Street ran from the city's heart—known as the Capital since all the Telvian government buildings were there—through all three districts. I imagined it like a target. The very middle was the city center, housing the Academy, Telvian Administration Buildings, and REG Command. Circling that was District 1, followed by District 2, and then 3 in concentric rings. The Telvian wall circled everything, cutting Telvia off from the rest of the UFA. Telvians believed that everything beyond the wall was nothing but desert and marauders. I knew the truth. An entire world existed beyond the wall…one I missed deeply.

There were few people bustling about, heading home from a long day as I walked down the street. I paid close attention too, looking at every person, hoping I'd come across Sally's mousy face. By the time I left the Capital and crossed into District 1, that little voice nagged me further.

Something's wrong. Something happened to her. Find her, Lin. Find her now*!*

I'm trying, I argued back. *Keep it together.*

I wondered if anyone else talked to themselves like I did?

After a few more minutes, I found myself walking the street alone.

"Shut the fuck up."

I stopped, listening hard, eyes scanning the street.

"Tim, please…" a soft voice cried. It was so low, so quiet, I wasn't even sure I actually heard it.

"Grab her." It came out as a low growl, and I knew it at that moment. I knew exactly who that voice belonged to.

Shit, shit, shit!

This section of Cameron Street was quiet except for the few muffled voices I was hearing. We were at the border of District 1 and 2. I scanned the buildings, trying to figure out where the voices were coming from until my eyes caught sight of a darkened pathway between two shops that were already closed for the evening.

There! Go! My intuition screamed at me. I didn't hesitate. I took off sprinting, turning the corner. The buildings blocked out the sun, making the alley darker than the rest of the street, but there was nobody there.

"Please, Tim," Sally whispered. "Please…whatever you want, just don't hurt me."

My heart jumped into my throat as I ran down the passageway.

I heard Harris chuckle menacingly. "You're Subclass Trash, Sally. There's nothing you have that I could want…except for one thing."

She screamed.

The passageway was actually a T, with another alleyway that ran parallel to Cameron Street. I slid to a stop, my navy-blue uniform flats skidding on the asphalt as I turned the corner. About halfway down was Sally being held by three other guys. Two of them held each one of her arms. I didn't recognize them. The third was the gangly dude from Mat 2. He had an arm wrapped around her waist while his free hand slammed down over her mouth, muffling her cries.

And Harris…

Tim-*fucking*-Harris…was approaching her like he'd just discovered a buffet.

"Hey!" I screamed out. I dropped my backpack to the floor. All four guys looked up at me. And Sally—poor Sally—her eyes glistened with tears. She was missing her glasses. God only knows where those were.

"Huang," Harris growled, deep and guttural.

"Get your hands off of her, or I'm going to hand you your own ass on a silver platter, Harris. And you too, Mat Two Boy. You're both going to eat *ass*-phalt." Then I chuckled. I couldn't help myself. "Get it? *Ass*-phalt? Because I'm going to serve your ass on a platter?" I chuckled some more.

They just stared at me.

Well, crap…that was no fun. "You guys are seriously lame," I groused.

Tim turned to face me head on, loosening his crimson-red uniform tie. "I'm going to enjoy this, Huang. I'm going to love making you pay."

I stared him down, my fingers itching to grab my daggers hidden under my skirt. But I couldn't blow my cover. Only if absolutely necessary.

"Let's dance, Harris. I'm ready."

6: Dance of Death

Tim came at me like a bull charging a matador. But just like yesterday, he was slow, and the key was to tire him out while keeping him from getting a hold of me. I may have been fast, but Harris was two times my weight and strong as hell.

I twirled, missing him completely, giving myself the opportunity to karate-chop his kidney just like I did to Gangles on Mat 2. This time, however, I hit him with everything I had. He yelped out, spun around, and swung his arm, trying to hit me. I ducked, popped back up, and snap kicked him. My foot hit his sternum and sent him stumbling backwards.

I laughed. "You're making it too easy on me, Harris."

He screamed and came barreling towards me again. I spun to the left, swung out my leg, and kicked him in the small of his back, sending him falling forwards to his face. *Idiot.* He scrambled to his feet.

"Enough of this ballerina shit, Huang," he scowled. "If you think you're so tough, come and get me," he said, motioning me forward.

I licked my lips, loving the burn of adrenaline and heat pumping through my veins. "All right, Harris. Time to send you crying home to your mommy."

Hands balled into fists and up to guard my face, I hopped on light feet with knees bent, ready to move. He stood there, mimicking my hands, but both feet remained planted flat on the ground like a damn tree.

Trees don't move. They come crashing down.

I came in hot and fast. His left arm twitched, tipping me off before he struck out with it. I ducked down, his left arm arcing over my head and leaving his left side open. I popped back up and—WHAM!—punched him in the nose. Harris's head snapped back as he stumbled backwards.

"Did that feel good?" I taunted.

"Bitch!" he yelled out as he tipped his face forward and touched the blood trickling from his left nostril. He glared at me and screamed, "Get her!"

Oh shit! I whirled around to face the guys behind me. Gangles held on to Sally, but the other two guys rushed me. I dodged Henchman One, but I couldn't dodge the other guy. Henchman Two came in with a sucker punch to my gut, just as Tim wrapped his arms around me and squeezed like a freaking vice. My stomach muscles spasmed as Tim lifted me off the floor.

"June!" Sally screamed, wiggling in Gangles's arms as he covered her mouth again.

Henchman Two came in close for another punch, but I kicked out, hitting him in the groin. He dropped like a swatted fly, cupping his crotch and whimpering. My eyes drifted to Sally once more as Gangles screeched out and let her go, shaking out the hand that had covered her mouth. She had bitten him.

Attagirl, Sal! "Run!" I screamed at her. Thankfully, she listened, dodging Henchman One as he leaped out to grab at her. "Go, go, go!" I chanted.

"Shut up!" Harris yelled at me, squeezing me even harder. I felt like a balloon on the verge of popping. "Leave her, Greg," he ordered.

Henchman One stopped his pursuit of Sally and turned back to face us. This was not good. Not good at all.

Your dagger! Reach for your dagger! My intuition demanded. Hands pinned down at my sides, I could feel both blades—Honor and Glory—dying to be used. Begging to taste blood. My finger fiddled with the fabric of my skirt, desperately trying to get underneath the pleats when Greg punched me.

"Yeah!" Harris cheered as my face went flying to the right. He squeezed harder. "Do it again."

WHAM!

Another hit, this time from the left. I tasted metal in my mouth, and my tongue instinctually went to lick the corner of my lip. Blood. The jerk split my lip.

"Again!" Harris ordered. But my fingers had finally found a dagger. I pulled it out and sliced Tim's thigh.

He screamed out, dropping me like a sack of potatoes. The minute my feet touched the concrete, I ran, slipping the dagger back into its sheath before anyone saw my weapon.

"The bitch cut me! *Get her*!"

I didn't even bother to grab my bag. Forget it. Four against one was not an even fight. I was good—*real good*—but I couldn't take on four guys without giving away my identity. Right as I began turning the corner, someone tackled me, and my face ate asphalt.

"Holy shit!" I cried, seeing stars from the impact. Someone grabbed my ankles, and then I was being dragged back into the seclusion of the alley. I blinked furiously, trying to clear the haze before finally making out freaking Gangles pulling one of my legs while Greg yanked on the other. I kicked out, throwing Mat Two Boy off balance and causing him to fall over. *Idiot!* But Greg kept pulling, my thighs scraping against the dirt, grime, and nastiness of the alley floor.

"Let me go!" I screamed out as I tried to kick him.

Harris was suddenly in my line of vision, and his booted foot came crashing into my ribs.

I cried out, curling onto my side.

"I'm going to murder you, Huang. You're *dead*!" Then his foot came flying toward my face as I closed my eyes and prepared for impact.

"Oof!" Harris groaned out.

My eyes shot open, and suddenly Harris was on the floor. Greg let go of my foot and I scrambled to get to my feet. Greg stood there, palms out in surrender, while Gangles was on his left and Henchman Two on his right. Harris was on the floor, crab crawling backwards towards his freaking goons.

And there, standing between me and my four attackers, was Javier de la Puente. He was still wearing his school uniform, but in his hand, he held a silvery stretch of pipe, about five feet in length. He twirled it around in one hand, maneuvering it with such expertise that I instantly knew this man had trained with a bo staff before. And god was it hot. His obsidian eyes found mine.

"¿Estás bien, mi vida?"

"W-what?" I seriously had to find this guy an English dictionary.

No humor on his face. No cocky grin. No laughter in his eyes. Nothing but hard lines of sexy, Latin badassery. "Are you hurt?"

My tongue licked the cut on my lip. "I'm fine," I groused.

Harris stood from the floor. "Javier...my man," he said cautiously. "I'm glad you're here."

Javier kept his eyes on me a moment longer, traveling the length of me. Calculating. Searching. When he seemed convinced, he returned his attention to Harris. "You're lacking a dick, Tim. What the hell is your problem?"

Tim's face turned red, and I swore steam was coming off him in curling wisps of anger born of what had to be embarrassment and frustration. He looked like he was about to explode. Pointing an accusatory finger at me, he roared out, "That bitch's a rebel, Javi! She cut me with something. She's got a weapon on her someplace, I *know* it!"

My heart thundered in my chest. This was so bad.

If Javier believed him...

If I got reported...

Keep it together, Lin. Stay calm. I swallowed, holding my head up high. "I don't know what he's talking about. They attacked Sally, and I was just—"

Without so much as a glance my way, Javier lifted his hand, silencing me. He took another step toward Harris, planting himself squarely in between me and the four guys. "Te voy a decir esto una vez nomas... I'm going to tell you this only once." He pointed the pipe at Harris. "Touch June Huang or her friend again, and I'll fucking kill you myself, Tim."

My jaw hit the damn floor. Did he seriously just give Tim a death threat? Holy crap!

Tim rolled his shoulders back, working his jaw like he was chewing glass. Javier met his stare head on before lifting his chin and speaking one single word.

"*Leave.*" It rumbled out of him—so deep, so freaking sexy—and I thought I was going to drop to my knees.

Tim nodded, still seething from his lack of power. He snapped his fingers, and his little gang of assholes walked past us, giving Javier a wide berth. He limped the whole way, and I watched as they rounded the corner, one by one vanishing into the adjacent alley. Tim paused for only a breath, giving me one last hard glare, and then disappeared.

My lungs ached as I blew out a breath I didn't even realize I'd been holding. My body felt like it was vibrating from the leftover adrenaline still pumping in my veins. I closed my eyes, taking in a deep breath and holding it. *One…two…three…four…*

A gentle touch on my chin caused my eyes to fly open and freeze. Javier stood before me, my chin in his hand as he tilted it to the side and scrutinized my face.

"That shithead hurt you," he muttered.

My heart pattered. Not pounded, but freaking *pattered*. Since when did my heart *patter*? "I'm fine," I whispered. *Pull away, Lin. Pull away now.*

I didn't.

I just stood there, allowing his eyes to warm my skin as they glided from my eyes to my mouth. His thumb glossed across my bottom lip, causing them to part, and I shivered.

Pull away! my conscience cried.

But I…I don't think I want to.

"Did he touch you anywhere else?"

"No." I sounded breathless. Oh my stars, what the hell was wrong with me?

"June!"

I snapped out of it, pulling away from Javier in time to see Sally running down the alley. "Sal?"

"Oh my gosh, June, you're okay!" She looked at Javier and clasped her hands in front of her like she was praying. "Thank you so much!"

The heat left his gaze as he looked at Sally. "Don't thank me," he said. "It wasn't a problem at all." He took a step back, discarding the pipe into a dumpster. "You're sure you're all right?"

I nodded just as Sally cooed, "Oh June, your lip—"

"I'm *fine*. Seriously, stop fussing," I groused. I turned my face to keep her from grabbing at it and sought Javier's gaze once more.

Casually, he tucked his hands into his pockets. "Nos veremos, mi vida," he said as he turned on his heels.

"*English*," I called out after him.

He chuckled, never looking back. "I'll see you around."

Heat blossomed within me, coloring my cheeks. And suddenly, my lips parted in a silent gasp as the significance of what had just occurred hit me like a damn train.

Javier de la Puente had just saved my life.

7: A Dangerous Road

I was in a daze the rest of my walk home. I made sure Sally crossed over into District 3 safely, and the whole time she just rattled on and on about how Harris had lured her into the alley, and how she thought she was going to die, and how I saved her, and how she ran for help and bumped into Javier on his walk home, and *blah, blah, blah.*

I knew it was her nerves making her go on like she was, but I had a massive headache, and I was two seconds away from stabbing my own brain with Glory to end the pain. Once she crossed over into her district, I was at peace, and I could finally think.

Freaking Javier de la Puente *saved* my life.

The nephew of the dictator I was trying to oust from power was the guy who came to my aid. And not only did he come defend me, he threatened Harris—a Noble Class citizen. Sure, Javier was Noble too. And not just any Noble, but a blood relative of the president. But *still*...Harris's dad was the general of the REG. I'm sure there would be consequences in some form if Tim told his dad.

But I think what puzzled me more was that he came to the aid of someone *below* him. I wasn't Noble. I was Middle Class. Sally was *Subclass.* Yet...he came to help *us.*

Why?

There was literally nothing for him to gain by helping us. Tim could have slaughtered me and Sally, discarded our bodies in a dumpster, and that would be the end of it. And yet, here comes *Rico Suave* twirling his stupid pipe, looking like a badass, speaking Spanish and shit like some sort of sexy fallen angel.

I mean, *who does that?*

I *hate* Javier de la Puente.

I hate *all* the de la Puentes.

They're bad, bad, *bad*!

And yet, Javier was not *bad*...was he?

If he was bad, would he have even given a Subclass citizen the time of day? And on the off chance he would—which he *did*—would he have risked his own status as a Noble by defending two girls below his caste if he was truly a bad guy?

Because he *did*. He did *both* of those things. And then he went all dark angel on me with that stupid sexy swagger and all that *"mi vida"* bullshit. I don't even know what the hell *"mi vida"* means!

He could be all like, *"See you around, donkey pie,"* for all I knew. And here I was, getting ready to drop my underwear because the jerk speaks a second language.

Well good for *you*, buddy. I could speak Spanish too. *¿Dónde está el baño?* There!

"Ugh!" I speared my fingers through my hair, trying to contain my confusion. "This day needs to be over," I muttered.

I was all too happy when I got home. But of course, I had to deal with May, who almost had a heart attack when she saw my face. My lip was only a little swollen, and the cut had stopped bleeding some time ago. Thankfully, May had an excellent first aid kit, compliments of the Dissenters. If we got hurt during a mission, we couldn't just waltz over to the hospital, now could we? Nope. We had to treat ourselves in-house.

An icepack, amazing anti-inflammatory creams, and two magic pills later, I was in bed getting rest. But no matter how much I tried to sleep, I just kept thinking about the way Javier touched me.

About how my skin tingled and ached for another brush of his fingertips.

About how his nearly black eyes lit a fire deep inside, low and hot.

About how the smell of him intoxicated me, curling into the furthest corners of my being.

I just kept thinking about Javier de la Puente, and I knew at that moment that I was in deep trouble.

★★★

Because of what happened on Wednesday, May and I maintained a low profile for the next twenty-four hours. May called me out of school, claiming I had a cold, and she didn't go to work on the account of having to take care of me.

Sally texted that evening to make sure I was okay, and I told her I just couldn't face Harris following the incident. She understood. She shared that the tension was thick between Javier and Harris, and that Javier must have told his cousin what happened. Apparently, the de la Puente cousins were walking the school like they owned the place, giving Harris and his goons no room to peacock around like they normally did. She said after school, Jacob showed up and escorted her home. That boggled my mind. I could practically hear her voice gushing in my head as I read her texts. Then she shared that Javier asked her if I was okay, and if I needed anything.

When I read that, I fell out of my chair. The look May gave me had me blushing and practically crawling back upstairs to my room.

> June: What did you tell him?
> Sally: I told him you were fine, and that he should leave you alone.

I almost chucked my tab across the room.

> June: Why would you tell him that?
> Sally: Because you hate him, right? Did I do the wrong thing?

When I read those words, I felt my heart plummet. Javier was a *de la Puente*. I *did* hate him, didn't I? I placed my hand on my forehead. Holy stars, what was I doing?

★★★

Friday I had to go to school. The cut on my lip was scabbed up, and the cream May gave me did wonders for the swelling, leaving behind only a little bruising. The same could not be said for my stomach. Those jerks got in several solid punches, and one good kick to my ribs and gut. Thankfully, nothing was broken. But my muscles ached, and my skin was mottled with bruising in all shades of green, purple, and black. Nobody would see it under my uniform, though, and I looked almost as good as new in my white blouse, red tie, and navy-blue skirt.

So off to school I went.

My first several classes dragged on. Sally and I shared only one class, while Chase and I shared the other two. Before class, he asked me why I was missing the day before, and I told him what happened. He looked like he was going to blow a gasket.

"Are you sure it was actually *him*?"

I scowled. "Do I look blind to you? Of course it was *him*! Who else walks around this place speaking a forgotten language like a telenovela star?"

His eyes drifted to the floor. Disbelief etched the lines of his face. "I just…I can't believe he helped you."

Twisted in my chair, facing him as we waited for class to start, I muttered, "That makes two of us."

Chase ran his fingers through his hair, eyes glazed over. "But you're *okay*, right?"

I nodded. "Just sore. But I'll be fine."

He nodded slowly. Then his eyes flickered and zeroed in on something behind me. "Speak of the devil."

My brows knitted together as I turned in my chair, only to be ensnared by a pair of obsidian eyes.

"Señorita Huang…" Javier's voice was like silk and smooth dark chocolate—rich and delightfully wicked. In compliance with school dress policy, he wore the same navy-blue slacks, white button-down shirt, and crimson-red tie as every other boy. But with his sleeves rolled up a quarter of the way, and the tie sitting just a hair loose around his neck…it was enough to say he had his own mind and his own identity.

"Javier…" His name fell from my lips in a whisper, instantly coloring my cheeks.

Are you seriously breathless right now? my intuition asked.

Shut up, I snapped back at it.

Javier's eyes scanned the length of me, and I suddenly felt exposed…*naked*. Finally, they rested back on my eyes as he tipped his head to the side. "Me preocupé ayer sobre ti."

My heart backfired like the engine of a beat-up truck. "English…please."

Yup. You sound breathless. Like some chick on the front of an old-school romance novel, that stupid little voice scoffed. I gave her the mental middle finger.

He smiled—and holy guacamole was it a beautiful smile—as he placed a hand over his heart. "Perdóname…"

God, his accent sounded sinful…

"Forgive me," he translated. "I forgot that you only enjoy the English language."

"I'm getting used to it," I replied with a slight purr.

WHAT? Did you seriously just tell him that? I could hear the disdain in that little voice.

Shut up! Shut up! Shut UP! I shot back. I briefly wondered if I had multiple personalities. Talking to myself the way I did couldn't possibly be normal.

"Then I look forward to the day you enjoy it," he said, eyes glittering as they reflected the light.

I grinned, my heart thrumming with restless energy.

The bell rang, and Watkins clapped her hands several times, calling our attention to the front. But I couldn't take my eyes off of Javier.

He ran his bottom lip between his teeth, then shook his head lightly. Bending down low, he brought his face within a foot of mine. "Hasta luego, mi vida." Then he straightened and walked back to his seat.

I blew out a breath, feeling dazed, until I heard Chase's voice in my ear. "You're blushing, June."

"I don't care *who* you are, Chase. I *will* cut you."

He chuckled, and all I could do was sink into my chair as he walked off to his.

You're walking down a dangerous road, Liddy Le, my intuition said as Watkins started lecturing.

"I know," I muttered under my breath. "I know."

8: Cat and Mouse

Mid-break couldn't have come fast enough. Halfway through the school day, we all had a chance to take a breath. Where I was from, this would have been lunch time. But here, since nobody actually ate food, it was an opportunity to pop your nourishment pills, drink some water, and then hang out until your next class. Initiates were lucky in that the last week before Initiation was a breeze. Coming to school these final few days was more of a formality, and since we had already taken our exam, we were given an extended, hour-long break.

Sally and I were sitting on the artificial turf in one corner of the field behind the Academy. On the right was a jungle gym, and all the littles were running in circles, swinging, or going down the slide. I leaned against the unrelenting trunk of a piss-poor imitation of an oak tree. None of the vegetation in Telvia was real. Only the succulents were alive. Everything else was a plastic replica.

"Your face looks so much better than I thought it was going to," Sally commented, scrutinizing my lip.

I pulled back. "Uh, thanks."

Her spare glasses slipped down the bridge of her nose. "Did I tell you that Tim apologized to me this morning?"

"*No.* Are you serious?" Now this was interesting. Tim Harris apologizing to a Subclass? That was…*weird.*

She nodded, pushing her glasses back up her nose. "It's true. I couldn't believe it. He found me at my locker and said he was sorry."

Interesting… I looked at the playground. A little girl in pigtails squealed as she went down the slide. As much as Sal totally deserved the apology, something about it didn't sit right.

Smack!

Sally hit my knee.

"Ow! What was that for?" I complained as I faced her. But she wasn't looking at me. She was staring off to the left behind me, eyes wide and shaking like she just discovered cheeseburgers for the first time.

You're literally the only person who loses their shit over meat.

It's delicious. You're just jealous, I snapped back. God, my conscience was such a bitch.

I turned at the waist, peering around the trunk to see what Sally was gawking at. It took me all of two seconds before I whipped my head back around, shaking my hands in front of me.

"It's him!" I squeaked.

"I know!" she squealed.

She thinks you're talking about the other dude.

I am!

Liar, the voice accused.

"Good afternoon, ladies. Mind if we join you?"

Sally looked like she was about to become unglued as she gazed up at Jacob de la Puente. "H-hi, Jacob." The poor thing stuttered.

I almost couldn't look up. *Almost.* But I did. And when I did, I felt exactly the way Sally sounded. Javier had loosened his tie further and had undone the top three buttons of his shirt. If the curl of black ink I saw peeking from that little V of exposed skin was any sign of what laid underneath the rest of his shirt, I seriously wanted first-row seats to the viewing.

"Hola, mi vida."

I wasn't even looking at his face. My eyes were fixated on that tiny glimpse of black. "You have a tattoo."

Oh, holy lord, my conscience groaned.

Javier looked down for a fraction of a second as though he was trying to see what I was talking about. Then his eyes caught mine, black as night. "I have two, actually. This one you can see," he said as he rotated his left arm, showing off a minimalist image of a single lotus flower rising from ripples of water on the underside of his wrist. "The other...well, un día te lo enseño." He leaned forward, lowering his voice into a seductive purr. "That means, one day I'll show you."

I was frozen.

Just stared.

Gawked.

Sally smacked me, and I jumped, shifting my gaze to her. Her eyes widened as she ticked her head, clearly telling me to *act cool.*

Shake it off, Lin.

"Hey...so, Sally, I have to return something to Watkins," Jacob said, rubbing his hand along the back of neck. "I was hoping you'd keep me company?"

"Sure!"

My hand shot out and grabbed her wrist. "No! Uh...we were going to, um...study," I blubbered out like a stupid, lame duck.

She pinched her brows. "Study what?"

I heard Javier snicker under his breath, causing me to turn my attention back to him. "And what are *you* laughing at?" I groused.

His arms folded across his chest. "De ti, mi vida."

"*English.*"

Sally took advantage of my distraction and hopped to her feet.

"Sally!" I screeched, switching my focus back to her and grabbing at her again.

I missed.

"Bye, June! I'll see you later." She was practically skipping away from me. I pursed my lips, glaring at her frolicking form.

Javier glanced at the pair over his shoulder, silent for a heartbeat. And then, "They look good together, don't they?"

Whoa...there was no way he just said that. "Are you...are you making fun of her?"

He glanced at me. "Why would you think that?"

I motioned my hand at Sally's tiny image off in the distance. "Because she's Subclass, and he's...well, he's *him.*"

Javier cocked a brow, arms still crossed. "And do you think that because she's Subclass and he's the First Son that they shouldn't be matched?"

Stop. Pump the breaks. Make a hard U-turn right now, my voice ordered.

That question was loaded. And saying *no* could cause him to label me as a Subclass Sympathizer—someone who was well on their way to becoming a Dissenter. I couldn't afford that kind of speculation.

"Yes." My chest tightened. The word felt like shards of a broken Christmas ornament in my mouth.

His eyes flickered, the smile gone. "Interesante."

I swallowed, needing to change the subject. "I'm guessing that means *interesting*?"

He smirked. "Correct." In one graceful motion, he dropped to the floor.

Oh no…oh no, oh no, oh no. "I-I didn't say you could sit here."

Oh, but you totally want *him to sit here, don't you?* I swear, if it weren't because my conscience was actually me, I'd stab her.

He stretched out his legs, crossing his ankles as he leaned back on the heels of his hands. "I don't remember asking for permission," he answered, cocking his head at me.

My lips pressed together, and suddenly, I was uncomfortable. I looked the other way, staring at the children playing. They were all equal there. The playground was the great equalizer. And then they would grow up, and it would all change.

"¿De qué piensas?" I gave him the side-eye, and he chuckled. "What are you thinking?"

"Why do you always speak in Spanish?" I countered.

He smirked, looking off in front of him. "Why did you answer my question with a question?"

I faced him. "Because my thoughts are mine, and they don't belong to you."

He nodded, pursing his lips as his eyes drifted to his lap. "Entendido." He looked at me as a wisp of sleek black hair fell forward, framing his eye. "It means, *understood*."

Oh stars, he looked so beautiful. I licked my lips and peeled my gaze off of him.

"I speak Spanish because it's my heritage. My father and mother were both Latin, and it was important to my mother that I never lose our family's culture."

I couldn't help myself…I looked at him again. His eyes glassed over as though he was seeing his memories played out before him. Then he tucked his chin to his chest. "She believed that language held the key to preserving our past. To preserve it well, you have to be able to speak and understand it. Too much is lost in translation," he added as he leaned forward, drawing up his leg, his arm wrapping around his knee. "When she died, Spanish was all I had left of her. So I speak it as often as I can, because I refuse to forget her. Our shared language is the way I can always remember and honor her memory."

My heart sputtered and then oozed. Here I was, always criticizing him for speaking Spanish, thinking it was just some way of getting a leg up on me. I never realized that speaking the language was his way of remembering someone he had loved and lost. I grimaced.

"I—I'm sorry." I couldn't believe this. I was apologizing to Javier de la Puente. I shivered. *Oh my freaking stars, what is happening to me?*

Chin tucked to his chest, he glanced at me, causing that swath of black hair to fall forward completely, covering one eye. "You don't owe me anything, Señorita Huang."

"Oh, I certainly do. If you knew half the stuff I thought about you, you'd probably chuck my apology back in my face."

He laughed, deep and rich. "Now I'm interested in knowing just how low you think of me."

I waved him off. "That's okay. The last thing I need is for the president's nephew to know I call him every nasty name in the book when I see him."

He leaned toward me, dropping his voice. "Just how nasty, mi vida? Should I be worried?" And then his voice got *real* low…and *thick*. "Or should I be turned on?"

I squeaked. I couldn't believe it, but I. Literally. Squeaked.

I felt like a mouse caught by a cat.

Except that I wasn't a mouse.

He wasn't a cat.

And he was damn fine.

He chuckled, looking smug as he rose to his feet. "Just do me a favor, June. Let me know when you're ready to share with me some of those thoughts in your beautiful mind."

"Unlikely," I answered as he stepped back away from me.

"Tengo fe, mi vida," he replied with a breathtaking smile. "I have faith." Then he turned around and walked away.

9: Initiation

Saturday was the Initiation Ceremony. I could have been dying of the plague and I would have been expected to show up. May and I went together, of course. She wore a nice, light gray pantsuit with a pink blouse.

I *hated* pink.

She was always trying to get me to wear pink.

Thankfully, as an Initiate, I was expected to wear white. White tailored pants. White blouse. White blazer. White robe. All white. Unfortunately, with white, you could see anything that wasn't *white* underneath, which meant Honor and Glory had to stay home. The presidential family was to be in attendance, and that meant extra security. I couldn't risk being caught with them on my person or in my belongings.

I felt naked without them.

The ceremony was being held in the gym because of the heat outside. May joined the collection of other parents in the bleachers while I filed in line with my peers, looking for an empty seat in the ocean of white folding chairs in the middle of the gym. There were so many of us, and we all looked the same. I couldn't tell who was who in the sea of people. I told myself I was looking for Sally and Chase. But if I was being honest, I was looking for Javier.

Eventually, the dean of the Academy stood at the podium at the north end of the gym, and we all quieted down, taking our seats. He said a few words, which I didn't even pretend to pay attention to. All I did was scan the faces, looking for my target.

"Good afternoon, Initiates."

I snapped my attention to the front of the room. Raúl de la Puente stood at the podium, brown hair combed back, mocha-colored skin, a neatly groomed short beard, navy blue suit and crimson-red tie. If we were continuing the honesty game here, he was quite handsome for an old dude—though not nearly as attractive as his wife. Belinda de la Puente stood beside him, and her son was a spitting image of her—blonde, blue-eyed, refined, crisp. She screamed *elegance* but whispered *danger* with every turn of her head or shift of her eyes.

I couldn't help but notice, though, that tucked in the back corner was their daughter, Mara de la Puente. She was younger than her brother by two years—same as Edith. She was a petite thing. Definitely pretty. But it was clear her family didn't want her seen or noticed—relegated to the back and off to the side as though she was nothing more than hired help.

I wonder if Chase has seen her yet. He had his eyes on *that* one. But if he had any hope of dating the president's daughter, he was going to have to land a position in District 1, and that was a tall order.

"And with that, let us proceed with the Presentation of the Initiates," Raúl said, throwing his hands up in the air. The room cheered.

One-by-one, he announced the name of a candidate, along with their district assignment, and new career. At first it was kind of exciting. I kept listening for names I recognized. But after a while, I collapsed into a puddle of boredom.

God, why can't they just send you a text with all your new info?

I started nodding off, my head slowly bobbing forward when I heard, "Sally Miller. District 2. Telvian Technologies and Neural Laboratory, Innovations Program."

I snapped to attention, sitting up straight to see if I could catch sight of her. She was sitting five rows behind me and practically skipped her way up to the podium to accept her white envelope with all her new information. She was promoted up to District 2. Her family would remain in District 3, but at least Sally had a chance for a better life.

Way to go, Sal! I didn't think she would be promoted, but she *was* wicked smart with numbers and phenomenal when it came to the sciences. It made sense she would end up there.

A few names later, I recognized another name. "Chase Beckham. District 1. Health and Wellness Department, Inmate Care and Rehabilitation Program."

Damn it, Chase. You nailed it! This was excellent. As a District 1 citizen, he actually stood a chance at being matched with Mara when the time came.

"Timothy Harris, Jr. District 1. Rebel Enforcement Group, Apex Rehabilitation Institute."

"Bleh." I stuck my tongue out. I didn't care what Sally said about him apologizing. Freaking Harris didn't need his ego to be any bigger. *Damn ogre.*

"Jacob de la Puente. District 1. Rebel Enforcement Group, REG Command."

I slumped back in my chair, crossing my arms. That was super expected.

"Javier de la Puente. District 1. Rebel Enforcement Group, Apex Rehabilitation Institute."

My back went ramrod straight as my eyes searched the sea of people. Javier was at least six rows in front of me. His black hair was a sharp contrast to his white robe, and the smile he gave his uncle as he accepted his envelope made my insides feel mushy.

I shook my head. *Mushy?* I could not afford to be *mushy*!

I cleared my throat, tearing my eyes away from him as he walked back to his seat. I seriously needed to get my head checked. Maybe when I fell and hit the asphalt, I got concussed. Yeah…maybe that was it. I should have May examine me—

"June Huang. District 1. Telvian Enforcement, Administration Building 2."

My jaw hit the floor.

Well, this is an interesting turn of events. Not only had I been promoted, but I was now going to be the equivalent of a police officer in Telvia.

Well, hot damn. Go me.

10: Orders

After the ceremony, May hugged me and congratulated me on my success. Sally found me, as did Chase, and we all hugged each other, excited for each one of our successes. Sally was just non-stop chatter, and at one point, Chase elbowed me and rolled his eyes. I snickered. After a bit, people started clearing out. May gave me a kiss—all for show, of course—and went home. I stuck around a little longer when my least favorite person had the guts to walk up to me.

"Hey, Huang," he called out.

I rolled my shoulders back and lifted my head up high. "What do you want, Harris?" Sally froze at my side, but Chase came to stand at my shoulder in solidarity.

Tim's eyes shifted back and forth, but he cleared his throat and set his gaze on me. "Look, Junie—can I call you Junie?"

I glared, tucking my chin in.

"*June*," he corrected. "I just wanted to say I'm sorry about how I acted the other day." He put his hands up, palms out. "I was out of line."

"*Way* out of line, man," Chase scowled at my side. I said nothing. I did not trust Tim Harris, and I would pluck out my own eyeballs before I did.

"I know, I know," he insisted. Then he clapped his hands together. "But hey, I want to make it up to all of you. My house *tonight*. Graduation party. My folks are leaving for a little weekend getaway, and the place is mine."

"Really?" Sally gushed at my side.

He winked at her. I almost slapped him.

"Really," he confirmed. "You're District 2, Sal."

Sal? Since when does Harris call her *Sal?*

"And everyone in District 2 and 1 is invited," he added with a smile.

She skipped beside me. "Thanks, Tim!"

He placed a hand on his chest, beaming at her. "Of course. It's the least I could do." He took several steps back and pointed one finger at me and another at Chase. "You guys, too, okay? See ya all there. Dress your finest!" And then he turned on his heels and walked away.

"Oh, my gosh!" Sally started hopping up and down. "I get to go! I get to go! I've never been invited, but now I'm—"

"You are *not* going to Harris's party. *Please* tell me you will not stoop so low."

She frowned. "Why not?"

I rolled my eyes, shoulders collapsing. "Sally, the guy's only inviting you because you're in 2 now. Not because he's had some sort of *Come to Jesus* moment and is suddenly a saint."

Sally's face crumpled. "You know what, June? You're right."

"Thank you—"

"And that's why I'm going."

My eyes almost came falling out of my head with them opened so wide. "*What!*"

"You don't know what it's like to be a Subclass citizen. Nobody respects you. You starve every day because they don't give you nearly enough nourishment pills. People die every winter because of the cold, and overheat every summer—"

"Sal—"

"No!" She shut me up. "Neither of you knows what it's really like. I'm in freaking District 2 now. And that means I get to be treated like I *matter*. And I'm going to Tim Harris's party because for the past thirteen years of my life, I got to watch everyone else go to parties while I got excluded because I lived in 3." Tears were brimming in her eyes, cascading down her cheeks. "So I'm going, June. And I don't care *why* Tim invited me. I'm going and that's final."

I lifted my hands up in surrender. "Okay…you're right. I'm sorry. I didn't mean to hurt your feelings."

Sally stared at me for a long time, and for a second, I thought she was just going to flip me the bird and storm off. But her frown softened, and she finally nodded. "Okay. I forgive you…but only if you go with me."

I closed my eyes, feeling every instinct inside of me twisting, telling me to tell her no and walk the other way.

"Junie, *please*...I don't want to go alone."

I shook my head. "Take Chase."

"Hey! Whoa, now,'" he protested. "I can't. I got family stuff tonight."

I cocked a brow at him. *Jerk...what a copout.*

Sally grabbed my hands, holding them with such desperation, I actually felt bad for her. "Please, June. Jacob's going to be there, and I need to know my best friend's got my back."

"Jacob?"

She nodded enthusiastically. "Yes! He's going with Javier, and I really want a chance for him to see me in a cute dress—"

Javier was going to the party. He was going to be there with all his *Rico Suave* Spanish bullshit.

"Yes. Yes, I'll go."

"Eek!" she squealed as she threw her arms around me and squeezed. "Meet me at Central Park at a quarter to six, okay?"

I couldn't speak. My mouth went dry.

"You're the best! See you in a few hours!" Then she twirled around and ran off to find her parents.

Holy stars and baby monkeys...what did I just get myself into?

***

I threw open the door to the house. "May!" I shouted out into the hall. "I need a dress like my life depends on it!" I raced up the stairs, shouting her name again. "May!"

I glanced in her room, but she wasn't there. "May? Where are you? I need a dress, pronto!"

"What? What? What?" she chanted from down below. Her head popped out of the hallway that led to the family room. "What are you shouting about?"

My hands gripped the banister as I looked down into the entryway below. "I need a dress."

She shook her head, brows pinched. "A *dress*? What on earth do you need a dress for?"

"I'm being dragged to a party."

"A *party*? Where?"

I dropped to the floor, clutching the banister railings like I was staring at her through prison bars. "Tim-*freaking*-Harris's place."

Her eyes widened for half a second and then she busted out laughing.

I glared at her. "It's not funny, May. I ha—"

"Hate that guy, I know." She chuckled again. "Oh, honey," she shook her head, placing her hand on her hip. "You hate everything."

"That's not true," I retorted, and then watched as she cocked a brow. "*Fine*," I relented. "It's true." I pulled myself up and looked down at her from over the banister once more. "Regardless, I need a dress. One I can conceal my daggers in."

She gave a wispy sigh as she smiled up at me. "So Cinderella is going to the ball?"

I narrowed my eyes at her. "Don't you start with me," I warned.

She tried to suppress another laugh before she pointed a finger in the air like an idea had just popped into her head. "I think I have just the thing."

"If it's pink, I'll stab you, May. I won't even feel bad about it."

"Oh, Liddy, I think you're going to *love* it."

***

It was red—*blood* red—with spaghetti straps and a V-shaped neckline. Lacy fabric wrapped around and hugged my waistline, then flowed out into a skirt that came just an inch above my knee in the front and dropped lower in the back. The flow of the skirt hid the knives attached to each thigh perfectly. As long as no one grabbed my legs, they'd be none the wiser.

But that shouldn't be a problem.

There was none of that stuff—touching, grabbing, kissing—happening in Telvia. No dating allowed until after your Initiation Ceremony. Following that, you could apply for a Match Permit, requesting the Telvian Council permission to date the person you were interested in. If they thought it a suitable match, then you were granted permission. It didn't get much more boring than that.

Come to think of it, no wonder the dudes around here ogled everything with hair, boobs, and a pair of legs. And the girls were no better—five seconds from dropping their underwear at the first set of pretty eyes. Everyone around here had to be so sexually pent up and frustrated, it really was no surprise.

I sighed, brushing out the last bit of my hair, deciding to leave it down. Then I grabbed my pointed black heels and slipped them on. A look in the mirror showed me I didn't look too bad.

Damn, I really do clean up pretty nice, I thought as I looked at my reflection over my shoulder, making sure my butt looked good too.

"Liddy!" May called. She sounded muffled through my closed door. I opened it.

"Yeah?"

"You have orders."

"Crap!" I hustled out of the room, taking the stairs two at a time and almost killing myself in my heels, before launching myself into the family room. May stood, motioning for me to sit on the sofa. I did as she suggested, and then watched as she placed a Holo Box on the coffee table in front of me. We sat together as the little light blinked yellow and then blinked green.

Sergeant Major Anthony Giza was one of the major players for the rebellion, answering only to the leader of the Dissenters. Getting orders directly from him meant the orders were serious, highly classified, and of the utmost importance. I had never received orders directly from Giza before, and from the way May gave me the side-eye as his image formed in the bluish light, she had never received orders from him either. Whatever task he was giving me tonight was going to be big.

"Good evening, Mrs. Huang and Miss Le." The hologram flickered. I could just make out his dark complexion, smooth and rich. It made the grays in his shortly cropped hair and manicured goatee pop.

"Good evening, Sergeant Major," May said. "What orders do you have for us?"

Something about how his face contorted gave me the impression that he didn't like what he was about to say, and it caused unease to pool deep inside me. "Raúl has been cracking down hard on Subclass citizens, and intel coming in from the reeducation camps suggests anyone suspected of rebel activity is..." he faltered, pressing his lips into a thin line for a moment before continuing. "Being subject to torture."

My chest tightened. "Oh shit," I muttered. May elbowed me—a warning to watch my tongue. The reeducation camps were nasty places. Starvation and solitude were a common tactic used to make people succumb to the Telvian Council's demands. A person's innate drive to survive was powerful. People would do almost anything. But torture? That was a new low, even for Telvians.

"The UFA Council has decided that Raúl's tactics must be matched with an equal show of force," Giza moved on. His face became a blank slate. "They want him to know that if he tortures the people, we will strike him just as hard, and cause him just as much pain."

I frowned. "And how do you plan to do that, Sergeant Major?"

"*Liddy*," May scolded under her breath. I ignored her. I wasn't trying to be rude. I was genuinely intrigued by how the Dissenters planned to make Raúl *suffer*.

Giza grimaced. But he quickly wiped the expression from his face, bringing back his collected, stoic mask. "We've been informed of a gathering occurring in District 1. A party for Initiates, correct?"

"Uh, yeah. Timothy Harris is hosting a grad party. Why?"

He cleared his throat before wiping his mouth with his hand. Then, he delivered my orders. "It has come to our attention that a person of interest will be in attendance at the party. Are you familiar with the president's nephew?"

"Yeess?" I drawled.

"Your mission, Miss Le, is to assassinate Javier de la Puente."

Well, fuck a monkey and feed me a banana. This was going to be a problem.

11: Party at Harris's Place

The hologram disappeared, and I genuinely thought I was going to have a heart attack. My job was to assassinate Javier at the freaking party. Giza gave May orders to prepare to evacuate the moment I gave her the signal that I had done it.

The lights are out.

That was the code. I was to text her "the lights are out," and she would know to be ready to hightail it out of Telvia tonight. Then May and June Huang's identities would be wiped from the system. Sure, people who knew us would remember us. But any actual record of us would be destroyed.

I had to kill Javier de la Puente.

The thought alone was causing my stomach to roil.

"May, I can't do this," I said.

"What?" She grabbed my shoulders and forced me to face her. "What do you mean, you can't? You have to—"

I shook my head vehemently. "I can't. I can't kill him—'

"Liddy," she scolded, gripping me by my arm and dragging me toward the entryway. "You have to. Failure to do so would be a dereliction of duty. You could be court-martialed, and then what would happen to your family?"

I froze, only able to continue staring at her. Completely mortified and chilled to my core.

"You have to follow orders, Lin. You're a soldier. An *assassin*. You *knew* your job would always be to assassinate someone in Telvia. It's what you were trained to do."

My chest tightened horribly. I didn't want to do this. "But he *helped* me…he helped *Sally*—"

"And now he's a REG officer, Lin. His *job* is going to be to sniff out people like you and me and *kill* us. Or did you forget that part? Did you forget that he's going to torture people like us? That he's going to murder people just. Like. *Us*."

Each word felt like a slap to the face because she was right. May was a hundred percent right.

Javier de la Puente might have saved me that day in the alley, but if he ever discovered that I was working for the Dissenters, he would kill me. And I couldn't let him do that.

I nodded.

"That's a good girl," May said, stroking my hair. "Just remember who he is, Lin. If you have any doubt, remember who he *is* and who he's going to *become*."

I pulled away from her. He was a de la Puente. And he was going to become a murderer.

I could do this. I could kill him.

I had to.

★★★

My stomach was a hot mess as I waited for Sally to show up. The best thing I could do was shove my mission into the darkest corner of my mind until it was time. It wasn't helping much though.

"June!"

I turned around and saw Sally racing my way across the park…and she was wearing pink. "Oh my stars…you look like cotton candy."

It took everything inside me not to groan at the sight of her. With her poofy pink dress, hair done up in pretty curls on the top of her head, and little white heels, she looked good enough to eat. But that shade of pink made her look too innocent in my book. Though I guess that was the problem—she *was* innocent. And she had her eyes set on impressing one particular guy.

"What's cotton candy?"

Damn it, damn it, damn it! "Uh, it's nothing. Just a phrase I use sometimes." *You are such an idiot.* I couldn't have made a more rookie mistake even if I tried.

Get your head in the game, Lin, my intuition warned.

Her eyes filled with concern. "Is it bad? Does it not look good on me?" she asked as she looked down at herself with a worrisome frown.

I grimaced. "No, Sally. It means *sweet*. You look really sweet."

Her eyes lit up. "Oh good. And, oh my gosh, you look *amazing*!" She stared down at her own dress once more and then back at me. "I can't compete with you."

"Stop," I ordered. Leaning forward, I took her hand and started walking toward District 1's residential zone. The early summer heat felt good on my exposed shoulders, but my thick, silky black hair hung loose and free, covering my bare back. I tried to just focus on walking, on the way our heels clicked on the asphalt.

She shook her head, eyeing me with shocked little eyes as I guided her through the streets. "Red is *definitely* your color, Junie. It just makes your hair standout. You look...you look like..."

"A succubus?" I supplied and then laughed at my joke. I kind of did. Give me some pretty black bat wings, and I was all kinds of temptress...and just as deadly.

The last thought made my stomach sour, and I grimaced, shoving all the nasty emotions back down.

"*No*," she pushed back. "I would never call you that. It's just...god, June, you're so pretty and *exotic* looking. I just look like everybody else, but you—"

"Will you *stop*? Keep this up and I swear I'll turn around and head home," I threatened. "Trust me, the *last* thing I want is to go to Harris's party." Truer words had never been spoken.

She giggled. "You're always so grumpy. You hate everything."

"I *revile* everything," I corrected, miffed that those words had been hurled at me twice now this evening. "It's *different*."

"Sure," she said dubiously. "Whatever makes you less cranky, Junie."

I glared at her. "I resent that."

"Of course you do."

Five different Enforcement officers stopped us on our way, demanding to scan our retinas to confirm our identity. Then they drilled us on why we were out of our districts. Normally, you couldn't cross district lines unless you were being escorted by someone in that district or had permission. I was District 1 now, but that didn't go into effect until Monday. The invitation for Harris's graduation party was our ticket out of trouble, and I knew this. But every time an officer stopped us, I thought for sure one of them knew what I was up to, and they were going to haul me off. But no one knew who I was, or what I was planning to do tonight.

I was the only one that knew my secret, and every step I took was a step closer to committing a crime I didn't know if I could go through with.

The Harris house was enormous. You could have fit three District 2 houses in it. The front was nothing but artificial turf and Council approved succulents, just like everything else in Telvia. From the outside, everything looked quiet, but when Sally knocked and the double doors swung open wide, I just about fell over from the bumping of the music inside.

It was a freaking zoo.

The place was packed to the gills with students graduating from the Academy. They didn't have alcohol in Telvia, not like us in the North. But that sure didn't stop them from partying. As Sally and I walked through the house, I saw it all. There were people meandering on the stairs, running around on the second story, and people gambling on the giant dinner table.

Somebody was smoking something, and my nose wrinkled at the smell of it. The couches had been shoved away from the center of the living room where girls and guys danced like tomorrow was going to be their bastard child. That was the one thing I didn't think I'd see at this party, and yet it was flipping *everywhere*!

One couple made out on the sofa. Another set looked like they were about to strip naked on the dance floor. Another pair was all hands and legs. A couple to the left were—

I averted my eyes as my jaw hit the floor. "I...I think that guy's missing his pants."

Sally laughed at me. "That would be a *yes*."

I stared at her, completely dumbfounded. "How are Harris's parents okay with this?" Because if anyone from the Telvian Council found out what was going on in this house, we would all be in deep—

"They're not home, remember? Mr. and Mrs. Harris are having a weekend getaway. That's why Tim planned the party for tonight while they were gone. They're supposed to be back tomorrow."

"Well shit, Sally. You didn't think to mention to me that this was going to be some sort of ridiculous orgy? I would have worn *pants*!" If it weren't because I liked the girl so much, I think I would have killed her right there.

Sally giggled. "Don't tell me that Miss Revile is scared of a few boys?"

I glared at her, crossing my arms. "I hate you."

She smiled sweetly, patting my head. "I know."

The room broke out in hoots and hollers as the attention shifted to new people coming into the room. I turned to see what new idiot joined the damn Bunny Party, and instantly wished I hadn't.

"de la Puentes are in the house!" Harris called out, hooting as he walked toward the newcomers.

"Oh my gosh!" Sally squealed beside me, grabbing my arm. "There he is."

Yes, there he was. Jacob de la Puente, First Son and heir to Telvia, marched in with blond hair and blue eyes that rivaled glaciers. He looked like really expensive champagne. But that wasn't the *he* I was referring to. The he *I* was talking about was right behind Jacob. Javier walked in with the same swagger, like he owned the place. And with those tight black jeans and black t-shirt, he was anything but champagne. He was like refined dark chocolate.

Smooth.

Bitter.

Too damn decadent to be good for anybody.

Harris reached out for a high five. "I thought you guys weren't coming?" Jacob glanced at Javier, and then reluctantly high fived Tim.

"Yeah, neither did we," Jacob replied.

When Harris moved to Javier, looking for a high five, all Javier did was cock his head back and slip his hands into his pockets, leaving Tim hanging.

Tim slowly put his hand down, cleared his throat, and then addressed Jacob. "Make yourselves at home, bro."

"We plan to," Jacob said easily as his eyes scanned the room, and then stopped dead on Sally.

Oh brother…

She was practically vibrating with excitement as Jacob walked toward us. I, on the other hand, felt every muscle in my body lock into place.

"Hey, Sally," Jacob said smoothly, giving her a rather charming smile.

"H-hi, Jacob."

I cocked a brow at her, holding back the desire to smack her upside the head.

He held out his hand. "Wanna dance?"

"Sure," she squeaked, making me wince for her.

Jacob suppressed a laugh, took her hand, and led her out to the middle of the room, right into the fraternization zone. I wrinkled my nose. *Nooo thank you,* I thought as I crossed my arms.

"You don't strike me as the party type."

My heart stuttered like a freaking engine misfiring. And suddenly every vein in my body was pumping fire. I turned and found Javier standing next to me. I took a step back.

"Te ves muy bonita, mi vida."

"*You.*" *No, no, no, no. I'm not ready.*

He smiled. "Me."

"You can't be here," I said like a dumb, stupid idiot.

"And where would you like me to go?"

"Anywhere but the same place I'm at." *Because I'll kill you, you gorgeous jerk.*

He held out his hands, looking around. "I was invited to the party just like you, was I not?" He leaned against the wall, hooking his ankle across the other, arms crossed. "I was hoping you would be here."

"You were?" Damn, he looked good like that. The way his black hair framed his obsidian eyes.

"Yes." He leaned forward, and everything inside me froze as his lips came right up to my ear. "I think of you often, actually."

He thinks…about me? Often? My chest squeezed as air refused to enter my lungs.

"I keep thinking about how I might convince you to share your thoughts with me."

Holy stars, the heat coming off him was intoxicating—warm lavender and hot cedar.

He whispered, lips grazing the shell of my ear. "For the record, I said you looked beautiful."

I snapped out of it. "What?" Did he seriously just say—

He pushed off the wall, unfolding his arms. "I said," he began as his fingers brushed my cheek, my throat closing up. With a smooth, practiced swipe, he tucked a strand of my hair behind my ear. "That you look beautiful."

Holy baby monkeys and bananas everywhere. His eyes hooked mine, and I felt like a moth to a flame. "Don't do that," I managed to breathe out.

As if it wasn't bad enough, he stepped closer, eliminating the space between us as he used the back of his finger to trace the line of my jaw. "Do what, mi vida?"

My heart thundered, pounding so hard that I thought for sure everyone could hear it. I had to kill this man.

He was a de la Puente.

He was a Telvian officer. And not just any Telvian officer, but a *REG* officer.

How many Dissenters would he torture once he got to his command post on Monday?

He was no good for anybody.

He was *bad*.

But he saved you. If he's so bad, why would he defend you? Why would he defend Sally?

My lips parted under his heated gaze, and the feel of him so close to me sent my skin tingling in anticipation. He smelled so good; looked so devastatingly beautiful. So many soft features and so many powerful lines at the same time.

"¿Mi vida?" His tone asked me something, while the look of his eyes on my lips demanded something else. The hand tracing my jaw followed the line to my chin. And when his thumb brushed my bottom lip, my entire body trembled.

Damn it. I couldn't do this. I had a job to do.

I shook myself, stepping away from him, breaking whatever damn spell he was casting over me. He had to die. I had to kill him. Failure to do so meant dereliction of duty. It meant I broke the oath I made to my faction. It meant dishonor to my family.

"I need some air," I breathed out, spinning on my heels, and running out the back door.

12: When Bad is Good

I couldn't believe this was happening to me. What the hell was wrong with me?

You watched him defend somebody that needed help. You saw him do exactly what you thought he was incapable of. Javier de la Puente isn't a bad guy. He doesn't deserve to die, my conscience tried to reason.

Shit. I ran out into the backyard, which was big enough to be its own private park. The hot summer air wrapped around me. I couldn't afford to think this way. It wasn't my place to decide. I was a soldier, and my family depended on me to help keep them fed. If I was court-martialed…

No, no, no, no! I speared my fingers through my hair as I looked for the darkest corner of the yard. There were people out here too, and I needed a serious moment with my thoughts. I followed the pathway winding through the succulents until I was lost in a far corner, hiding behind a shed, finally by myself.

"You've got to get a hold of yourself," I mumbled as I buried my face in my hands. "There's no other way. You've got to do this." I stared at the floor, curling my hands into fists.

But you can't, the little voice in my head pleaded.

I have to! I argued back. *He'll end up hurting so many others.*

You don't know that. He saved you!

"Erg!" I shrieked. "*Stop* it. It ends tonight!"

"What ends?"

I spun around so fast, my hand already reaching for Glory, but stopped the second my eyes landed on *him*.

"Damn it, Javier!" My fingers itched. I could do it now. One quick swipe to grab Glory, and a flick of the wrist would send my blade singing through the air and right into his heart.

It would be quick.

It would be painless.

It would be done.

He lifted his hands, palms out in surrender. "Perdóname. I only wanted to ask for your forgiveness."

"My *what?*" *You have got to be kidding me.*

His eyes looked black in the moonlight as shadows played across his face. And—oh freaking hell—he looked so beautiful. Like a fallen angel leading me astray from my path of duty and righteousness.

"I shouldn't have touched you, mi vida." He stepped closer, my muscles coiling tight. "I should have asked your permission first."

"Are you for real?" I spat out at him. First, he saved me, and now he was being *chivalrous?*

Another step, hands still up, approaching me like a frightened doe. If only he knew I wasn't the one being hunted. I wasn't the one about to die.

"As real as the blood pumping through my heart." He took another step, bringing himself within range of my arms. I could touch him if I wanted. I could grip the collar of his shirt and pull him into me. But I didn't need to. Javier brought himself within a few inches of me, and I could feel the heat rolling off of him—the energy of his body intoxicating and sinful.

I could slit his throat, I told myself. *It would be easy.* With him this close, he would never notice my hand. My heart fluttered in my chest and adrenaline burned through my veins. Slowly, my right hand lifted the hem of my skirt, reaching underneath for Honor.

"I want to touch you," he whispered, his minty breath curling over my cheeks. I could almost taste it. My lips parted, bringing the smell of him into my core. "Do you want me to?" His voice was like a spell, and I was falling under it.

I swallowed. "Yes," I uttered as my hand gripped the hilt, dragging it out of its sheath.

The back of his finger grazed my cheek as his eyes searched the lines of my face. "Te quiero besar, mi vida."

My grip tightened on the hilt, preparing to strike. My heart was beating so fast, I swore it was going to give out. "Wha—what does that mean?" I could barely speak. My words came out breathless.

The fingers of both his hands followed the line of my jaw, burying themselves in my hair. And the way he held my face—the tender way he cradled me—I thought my heart was about to explode.

"It means I want to kiss you."

Time stood still.

It ceased to exist.

I couldn't breathe. I couldn't think. I was totally and completely lost.

So many emotions were swirling inside me.

So many feelings drowning my heart.

So many sensations cascading through me.

A spell. This was a spell cast by foreign words, strung together and sung to me like poetry. And bless the stars, I wanted it. I wanted to fall under. I wanted to dive deep and never come back up for air. His lips were so close, I thought I could actually feel the energy of them hovering over my bottom lip.

His nose grazed my cheek, and then caressed my own in the gentlest way, as though I might break if he even whispered too loudly. "I want to kiss you, June," he said again, declaring his intentions with every word uttered like a prayer to the divine. And when he spoke next, I felt the suppleness of his lips brush mine with each word. "May I?"

My chest was so tight—so achingly, deliciously tight.

I wanted...

I *needed*...

He couldn't be bad when he felt so good.

This couldn't be wrong when my heart sang that it was right.

Oh freaking hell... "Yes."

Javier's lips met mine, and the moment they did, my knees threatened to buckle. Minty coolness filled my lungs, and when his tongue grazed my bottom lip, my traitorous mouth parted. In one fluid stroke, I tasted him. My free hand drew up to his chest, gripped the fabric of his shirt, and then I was lost.

I was gone.

Javier walked me backward, lips never leaving mine, and I dropped Honor to the floor in a muted thud. My back hit the border wall of the yard, and I was deliciously trapped.

He was hungry.

He was demanding.

And I was no delicate thing.

I nipped his lip, causing him to startle against me for only a moment before a primitive sound escaped him, egging me on.

His hand was in my hair, pulling it back to expose my neck, and then he was kissing and biting and sucking and sending sinful shivers across my skin. My fingers pulled on his shirt as his mouth trailed up my throat, along my jaw, and found my lips once again.

I couldn't do this. I couldn't be here. I was supposed to be *killing* him!

But my fucking stars, he was beautiful. And he tasted so good, felt so delightfully decadent against me. My hands were in his hair. My tongue was caressing his. And I was melting into a puddle of hot and heavy want.

This wasn't fair. None of this was *fair*.

His hand traveled down my neck, over the swell of my chest, until it gripped and kneaded my left hip. "Quiero más, mi vida… I want more," his voice was thick and husky. Nothing more than ragged breaths.

I arched against him, and the sound that erupted from his throat was guttural and so sinfully pleasing to my ears. My body had a mind of its own, and the sounds coming from him made me respond with pure, raw instinct. My left leg rose, causing the skirt to drift up my thigh. It was an invitation that needed no words. The soft touch of his hand landed on my knee, and then crept up my thigh, leaving a trail of heated flesh right as he came up to—

Glory! Shit!

I slapped his hand away, but it was too late. No sooner did I smack his wrist did he grip the hilt of my dagger and yank it out.

"No!"

He backed away in one fluid step, holding up the blade with a scrutinizing gaze. "¿Y esto?"

My whole body went rigid as stone, chest tightening as though a vice had gripped and squeezed. "I can explain…" What the hell was I going to *explain*? I was dead. I was so dead it wasn't even funny.

His brows drew forward in a sinister twist as his black eyes bore into me. "Who the fuck are you?"

I raised my hands in surrender. I had no options. I couldn't run. I couldn't fight. I had lost both my daggers. *Holy stars, I'm going to die.* I blew my stupid cover like an idiot because the dude kissed me. What a freaking moron I was. "Javier…it's not what you think," I tried feebly.

The scowl on his face would have caused Harris to piss his pants. "*Really?* Because right now, it looks like you're carrying contraband on your person, Huang. And it *really* looks like you're a fucking rebel."

I swallowed. "I-I'm…" I was stuttering. Nothing was going to give me away like stuttering. But what the hell was I going to say? Even if I denied being a rebel, I was still in possession of weapons—a major, major offense in Telvia, with consequences determined by the REG. I switched tactics. "Javier, *please*…" I was begging now. I was going to grovel for my life.

He ran a hand through his hair as he paced. "Fuck," he snapped out. And then pointed the dagger at me. "You *are* a rebel, aren't you? Harris was right. You cut him that day, didn't you? With *this*," he accused, brandishing my knife.

I swallowed, keeping my hands up. I didn't dare move. "*Please*," I whispered again. My vision blurred, and a single tear rolled down my cheek.

Then a shout broke out through the yard. "REG! The REG's here!"

Javier never took his eyes off me. "Y ahora viene tu jurado."

My breaths were so shallow, I could hardly form words. "What does that mean?"

He narrowed his eyes as he translated. "Here comes your jury."

I was dead. This was it. My time had finally come, and there was nothing I could do about it. Everyone here was freaking out because they were out past curfew and practically having an orgy in the damn family room.

Were they going to be in deep shit? That was a hell yes.

But no one was going to die for it.

But *I* was.

I hung my head. I would never see my sister again. I would never see my family, or my friends, or eat another cheeseburger again. All because of one forsaken kiss.

"Go."

My head shot up. The look on Javier's face was so pained, so twisted in confusion and debate, I didn't even know how to handle it. "What?"

He narrowed his gaze. "Go! *Vete!*"

My jaw dropped. He was…he was letting me *go?*

"In the back left corner, there's a garden gate to the alley," he explained, taking another step back from me. "Now go, or they'll catch you." Then he pointed my dagger at me once again. "But if I ever see you within Telvia's borders again, Huang, I'll turn you in myself."

I trembled.

"*Go!*" he yelled at me.

I ran. I rushed through the yard looking for the gate, found it, and launched myself into the alley. I raced through the night. I had to make it home. I had to tell May our cover was blown.

Javier de la Puente saved my life.

Javier de la Puente let me *live.*

And I never even said *thank you.*

★★★

"May! The lights are out! The lights are out!" I screamed as I launched myself into the house. "We gotta go! May!" I shrieked again. "We've got to go *right now!*" I threw my high heels into the corner and took the stairs two at a time. "May!" I screamed again. "They know who I am! They figured it out!"

I ran into her bedroom, but the bed was empty. I whirled around. *Where the hell is she?* "May?" I ran into my room, but it was empty too. Racing out, I started down the stairs and back into the entryway. "May?"

"Out past curfew, Miss Huang?"

I twirled around, eyes landing on a man with graying hair, a navy-blue uniform decorated with stars, and white stitching that read *R.E.G.*

"Oh shit," I muttered out.

"Indeed," he said as he stepped into the entryway. Behind him stood two more REG officers and a woman with a brown sack over her head.

"May…" My heart thrummed. My pulse vibrated with such intensity, I thought my skin was going to shake off my bones.

"It's over, Dissenter," the man announced. "Time to answer for your crimes."

I spun around to race out the door, but before I took my first step, a bag was thrown over my head.

WHACK!

And then the lights truly went out.

13: Prisoner JH4456

My eyes fluttered open, but I wished they hadn't. It felt like a spike had been driven through my skull. I groaned. Something was digging into the back of my head, hard and unrelenting. My vision was blurry…never a good sign. I blinked a few times, drawing my hand up to rub them.

I couldn't.

Panic seized me.

I tried moving my arms again, but felt pressure digging into my wrists. *Oh no…* I blinked several more times, trying to lift my achy head, trying to move my legs.

I couldn't move them either.

Something dug into the skin of my ankles. But my head responded. Reluctantly, painfully—but it moved. Agonizingly sharp fingers clawed into the muscles of my neck and upper shoulders, reminding me of when I would wake up sore from sleeping wrong. I hissed with each shift as I tried to open my eyes wide, the blurriness slowly shaping into shades of black, gray, and dark browns. Lines of shapes—bends, curves, pointed edges—slowly growing in clarity, until finally I could see the trouble I was in.

And I *was* in trouble.

Big, deep, piles of shit kind of trouble.

I looked around, wincing as the muscles in my neck protested. I was in a metal chair—wrists tied to the armrests and ankles bound to the legs. A drain rested between my feet, splattered with drops of brownish red.

Oh freaking stars…is that dried blood?

I remembered Giza saying that the Telvians had escalated to torturing their captives. My stomach roiled, causing me to wretch, but of course, nothing came out. Nothing but a heave and that disgusting feeling of nausea. I shivered, and my bindings dug further into my flesh.

Keep it together, Lin. Stay with it, the little voice coached. Closing my eyes, I breathed in slow and deep through my nose, settling the unease in the pit of my stomach, and then released it gently through my mouth. *Good. Now assess.*

Opening my eyes once more, I continued studying my surroundings.

A solid steel door was directly in front of me. The room had no windows, only a measly lightbulb that cast shadows along the dark gray stone of the walls, floors, and ceiling. It was punctuated with the similar dark hues of burgundy and shades of brown as the drain.

More blood. *Old* blood.

Where was May?

My heart was a mustang racing in the west. A relentless galloping that pumped blood and fueled tingling heat from the tips of my fingers to the southern points of my toes.

I was alone. I was in trouble.

And there was no help coming.

Dissenters didn't negotiate with Raúl because Raúl refused to negotiate with terrorists.

No help was coming for me.

No rescue.

No salvation.

No hope.

I was alone.

And then my little light went out.

★★★

When there are no windows, you can't see the sun. And when you can't see the sun, you can't watch the days pass.

Seconds meld into minutes.

Minutes melt into hours.

Hours blend into days.

Except time doesn't exist anymore.

Time keeps ticking, but the seconds mean nothing. Just echoes of memories. Fractions of moments. Shards of existence that don't come or go, but simply disappear.

Loneliness was heavy.

The darkness was oppressive.

Hunger was a gnawing ache.

It wasn't long before depression settled in, and any glimmer of hope shattered into wisps of light that faded into nothingness.

I was alone.

And I was going to die alone.

★★★

The sound of metal grinding against metal was a bitter sharpness that made me cringe. I longed to cover my ears. To block the sound that was too loud after hearing nothing for an eternity. The light from the hallway flooded the space, and I sealed my eyes, pained by the brightness.

Muted steps of rubber shuffling against stone.

I tried to open my eyes, but the light was still too painful. Too overwhelming. I slammed them closed again.

"Prisoner JH4456, sir." One voice. Forceful. Male.

"Thank you." Another voice. Older. Grating. Also male. "And fix that light, private." A pause. "Prisoner JH4456..." The sound of a tap. "Ah, *June Huang*, is it? Open your eyes, Miss Huang. I like to look into the eyes of every rebel when I meet them."

I did as I was told. With a pinched face, I forced my eyes to open, cringing as I did.

"There we are," the man said. I blinked fast, trying to help my eyes adjust to the blinding light. "Well, Miss Huang, you certainly surprised us all."

He came into focus, and my face blanched as I saw him. "General Harris?" My voice came out hoarse from lack of use and dehydration.

"Good. You recognize me then." He looked so much like his son. Same storm gray eyes, dirty blond hair, and built like a freaking tank. The man had abnormally broad shoulders, and a chest like a barrel. His neck was the size of an entire baby.

If Tim was a tree, then this man was a damn sequoia.

Unlike Tim, however, General Timothy Harris, Sr. was clean shaven, and sported a scar that ran the length of his cheek. It had to be half an inch thick at its widest point. Somebody, or some*thing*, must have butterflied his face like a damn filet mignon steak.

The general snapped his fingers, and the soldier standing guard dragged in a metal chair. "Thank you, private." He reached for the backrest and pulled it into place across from me. With a little tug at the thighs of his pants, Harris sat down and made himself comfortable. "You know, Miss Huang, when Tim came home babbling that he suspected you were carrying contraband, I almost didn't believe him."

That's how they figured you out, Lin. Knifing Tim was a mistake, the little voice chided.

Yeah, only if I hadn't *cut him, he would have killed me right then and there*, I snapped back.

Something tells me that *fate would have been preferable.*

"I thought he did something stupid, something illegal." The general crossed his leg, resting his left ankle on his right knee. "But then when the doctor examined the wound on his thigh, it was indeed consistent with a blade."

I noticed the light bulb in the corner being replaced. Shifting my legs, I no longer felt the straps of my sheaths on my thighs.

"Now, we didn't find any knives in our search, but we found several other items that appeared to be suspect." Harris snapped his fingers, and the soldier brought in a metal tray filled with an assortment of items. "This, for example," he said as he lifted my Northern tab, "is not regulation. But when we tried to unlock it, it appeared to have self-destructed." He tsked. "Such a shame." He dropped it back into the box. Picked up something else. "Then there was this Holo Box…also not regulation. But this device seems to have wiped its own memory." He dropped it back in the box. "Useless…"

They have nothing. Other than Tim's accusation and two unregulated pieces of tech, they've got nothing to prove you're a Dissenter. My intuition sounded just as surprised as I felt.

Placing his left foot back on the floor, he shifted and crossed the other. "Now, Miss Huang, I want to work with you here. I'd hate to see such a promising Initiate lost for no reason. Tell me who you are and what your orders were. Cooperate, and I'll see that you are pardoned for your crimes against Telvia."

I tried to swallow. My lips were chapped, and my mouth felt like every inch was coated in baby powder. "I don't know what you're talking about, sir."

He chuckled, the sound a deep rumble in his chest. "Lying will not help your situation. Right now, I have a suspicion, and that is enough for me to hold you here. Cooperate, and things will go well. Choose to lie and be obstinate...well, things might not end favorably for you."

There was no way that admitting my associations with Dissenters was going to end *well* for me. That was a load of crap. My best chance of making it out of here alive was to keep my damn mouth shut and play the innocent card.

"General Harris, sir, I'm a citizen of Telvia. I would never do anything against—"

SMACK!

My face went flying to the right, sending my entire body careening to the floor. I tasted metal in my mouth, my face flat against the cold stone.

"That's all right, Miss Huang. We'll get to the bottom of this. One of you will speak, I'm sure of it."

My eyes widened. *May.* Would May take the bait?

I heard the metal chair scrape against the stone. "In the meantime, I'll make sure you're comfortable. Good day, Miss Huang." Rubber shuffled against stone. Metal ground against itself, and then the sound of a door closing.

I was alone.

They didn't even bother to sit me back up. I was on the floor, face pressed against the grimy ground. My tongue licked the corner of my mouth, tasting the blood.

You're in trouble, Lin, my intuition stated, as if it wasn't obvious.

I know! Just let me think...

If you can't find a way out of this, you're as good as dead—

Would you just shut up! If you can't be helpful, then bug off, I ordered.

The little voice stayed quiet.

Thank you.

The sound of the door greeted my ears again, but the angle I was at made it so I couldn't hear what was happening.

"Lift her up." A new voice. Male. Deep.

The shuffling of boots and then the soldier the general kept snapping at was in view. He grabbed me and sat me upright. I exhaled, grateful to be off the floor.

"Miss Huang?"

I turned my face and almost died when I saw him. "Chase?"

His expression was nothing but a blank mask. "I'm here to assess your health, Miss Huang."

I pinched my brows. "Assess my health?"

No matter how hard he worked to mask his emotions, he couldn't hide the look of sorrow in his eyes. He nodded. "Yes, miss."

"Why?"

His lips parted, but his voice failed him, if only for a moment. Then he cleared his throat and rolled his shoulders back. "I need to make sure you're fit for the interrogation process, Miss Huang. You've been selected for a research study in the Inmate Inquisition Program."

My face blanched.

Oh, holy freaking stars… I was going to be tortured.

14: I Know

With a REG officer standing guard, there wasn't much to say to him. But I asked questions I figured were benign enough that no one would later claim he was in cahoots with me. Because that was the problem. Now that I'd been caught and suspected as a Dissenter, anyone who had associations with me was going to be looked at with scrutiny. Chase and Sally were both in danger, and Sally was the one at greatest risk since she was already a former District 3 citizen. When I asked about her, Chase explained he hadn't seen her since Monday, which worried me.

And May...poor May... She had no chance. May was going to suffer through whatever they had planned for us just as much as I was. It took everything within me not to crumble for her.

I was released from the chair. Chase gave me water to hydrate, and I drank it greedily as he conducted a basic exam and answered my questions. I'd been missing for four days. On Monday, everyone reported to the Telvian Administration to begin the first day of their careers. Chase had been assigned to the Health and Wellness Department, specifically to the Inmate Health and Rehabilitation Program. That's why he was here. I was on his roster of patients to monitor. While he spoke to me, all I could do was send a million *thank yous* to the stars for offering me this one small kindness.

Other than dehydrated, Chase found me okay. "Damn it, June," he whispered so low, I almost couldn't hear him. "I—I don't know what to do. You're in deep shit."

"Shh," I shushed him as I put my shirt back on. "Don't you think I know that?"

With a deep frown, his green eyes flickered like blades of grass in a breeze. "What did you do? How did this happen?"

I peeked over his shoulder at the guard, who looked bored, then looked back at Chase. "Tim." His name sounded like nails on a chalkboard to my ears. "Tim told his dad about that day in the alley. He said I cut him."

The color drained from Chase's face. "Oh, June."

"Stop it," I scolded. "It doesn't matter now. I'm here, and I need to find a way out." I glanced over his shoulder again, but the guard still looked like he was about to fall asleep. I turned back to Chase. "Will you help?"

His lips pressed together, and I could see the war inside him playing across the lines of his face. It was a big ask. A dangerous one. One that I didn't expect him to say *yes* to. And if he said *no*, I wouldn't hold it against him.

He inhaled slowly. Drew his face closer to mine. "I'll always help you, June. You're my friend. Whatever the risk to me, I'm with you."

It took everything inside me not to hug him. Chase was truly an amazing man. I blinked several times, trying to clear the tears welling up. "Thank you," I whispered.

He pretended to input notes into his tablet. "I don't have all my clearances yet, and they know you and I were friends in the Academy. I think that's why they assigned you to my roster…to see how I react."

"Sounds about right. Is…" I hesitated. "Is May on your list too?"

He shook his head. "No. Someone else has her." He placed his hands on my throat and started feeling around. "I'm going to have to lie low for a while. Make sure they don't suspect me."

"Got it."

Another glance over his shoulder before he looked at me once more. "It's not going to be pretty, June. Whatever they have planned for you, stay strong."

Fear needled in my gut, but I shoved it down. "Don't worry about me. I got this." I was a soldier, trained for war, trained for pain. I could do this.

His arm twitched. The corner of his mouth quivered. He wanted to hug me. But he had to stay strong, too. No matter what he saw, he had to keep it together just as much as I did, rebel or not.

With a final nod, he whispered, "I'll be back. Just hang in there." Aloud, he announced, "I'm done." And then he walked out, leaving me alone in my new personal hell.

No one came after that. I laid on the floor with my moth-eaten blanket for a while and tried to sleep. In the evening, I was offered water and one nourishment pill—half the dose of what someone like me should take—but I gladly accepted it. I was going to need it. Whatever was coming next wasn't going to be pretty. But I couldn't crack. I couldn't break. Whatever they did, I had to resist the temptation to tell them anything. Because breaking meant betrayal of my region, dishonor to my family, and placing my friends and family at risk. I had to stay strong. I just had to.

***

The whine of my cell door splintered the quiet, making me cringe in the corner of the room. I opened my eyes as two men wearing navy blue REG uniforms entered my cell. Under their shirts, I suspected they were wearing level-1 armor at the minimum, protecting their vital organs from stabbings or smaller caliber bullets.

"Get up," Officer Ugly sneered.

I pulled my blanket back and slowly rose to my feet.

"Hands behind your back," he ordered.

I smirked. "Now say *please*…"

SMACK!

The other officer backhanded me so hard I actually stumbled back against the wall.

"Son of a—"

"Turn around *now*," Officer Jackass barked. "Or I'll hit you again."

I glared at him, resisting the urge to touch my face. *Don't be a smartass, Lin. This is going to be a rough day. Let's not give them more reasons to kill you before Chase has a chance to help*, the little voice chided. She was right, of course. That stupid voice was always right.

I pushed off the wall and did as I was told. Binders snapped onto my wrists, and then I was whipped around.

"Move it." Jackass shoved me forward as Ugly led the way.

It was a labyrinth, with hallways hewn from stone and air so thick with a cold and dank humidity that it sent a shiver down my spine. The rough surfaces of the walls bore the marks of meticulous carvings, feeling more like a mine than a prison.

I'm underground, I thought to myself. *That's smart.* Real *smart.*

If we're underground, then we've got to be at least thirty feet, my intuition answered. *No one will be able to track you down here.*

An oppressive sense of foreboding slithered into my core. *I know.*

The corridor stretched ahead and weaved left, with solid steel doors lining one side, and nothing but stone framing the other. The yellow glow of utility lights mounted along the ceiling illuminated the tunnel. Bundles of cords and cables snaked along the roof of the hallway, connecting each light to the next. Each caged light cast uneven shadows, and the yellow hue reflected off the cold, metallic surfaces of the doors. The silvery glint, coupled with the stone surroundings, heightened the sense of trepidation growing inside of me.

It's like a dungeon, the voice remarked.

It's not like *a dungeon*, I answered. *It* is *a dungeon.*

We're going to die down here, aren't we?

I couldn't answer the question. There was no use in arguing with the little voice. My intuition was always right. *Always.*

Finally, Officer Ugly pulled up in front of a door, similar to all the others. But this one had a black key fob to the left of it, right under a placard that declared *Interrogation Room 4*. Ugly flashed a card at the device. It blinked a yellow light twice and then blinked green. I heard a click and then a buzz, and then the officer grabbed the handle and opened the door.

This is it, Lin, the voice said. *Whatever happens, say nothing.*

"I know," I whispered under my breath. "I know."

It was all I could muster.

It was all I could say.

It was time.

15: Interrogation Room 4

General Harris watched me under a scrutinizing gaze. "Prisoner JH4456," he drawled. "Miss Huang…" It was like he was tasting the sound of my name, feeling the letters as his voice reverberated in his throat. "We'll start simple. Level 1 is the most gracious, my dear. I recommend you take advantage of this stage."

I narrowed my gaze at him. I was strapped into a metal chair, bolted on a dais. My arms were bound to the armrest at the elbows and wrists with unyielding leather straps. My legs had been similarly strapped to the chair at the knees and ankles. A metal collar wrapped around my throat, cold and relentless, keeping me from moving my head in the slightest, while electrodes had been placed on my temples. One other had been planted over my heart, under my shirt.

Arms behind his back, General Harris stepped up onto the raised platform where I was trapped in the dead center. "Now, as much as I would love to see how the adjustments to our programming play out, I want to be fair. We'll start with just simple questions. If you answer truthfully, we just move on to the next, and so forth." He clapped his hands and rubbed them together. "Simple enough, yes? But if you lie…well, that's where things might become a little uncomfortable for you. For your sake, Miss Huang, I do recommend you tell the truth." He looked so sincere, as though he genuinely cared about my comfort.

It was unnerving.

"Well, let's not dally. Are we ready to begin?" He looked to the far corner behind him.

A man in a lab coat worked at a standing desk, staring at monitors that glowed hues of blue and green into the glasses on his face. The man gave the general a thumbs up.

"Good." General Harris looked at me once more. "Remember, my dear, this is level 1." He turned and stepped off the platform, walking behind a yellow and black caution line painted on the floor that spanned the length of the stone room. Placing his arms behind his back once more, he turned to face me. "Are you ready to begin, Miss Huang?"

I said nothing.

"I'll take that as a *yes*. Now, first question. What is your name?"

I remained silent.

He waited. One second…two seconds…three seconds. "Now this doesn't work if you don't at least try to play along, my dear. Let's try it again, shall we? What is your name?"

I pressed my lips together, refusing to even look at him.

He tsked. "Doctor, would you please?"

I saw the man in the lab coat nod, and then tap something on his computer screen. I heard a whirring sound, a light flashed, and suddenly…

I was zapped with the sharpest sting of pain—like when you lick the end of a rectangular 9-volt battery—that shot through my entire system. Every single blood vessel was consumed by an electrical shock that made me inhale one sharp breath. But it was gone just as fast as it came. Quick, like a blink of an eye.

General Harris's face tilted slightly as his concerned gaze watched me. "How did that feel, Miss Huang? Unpleasant, I would imagine."

My heart stuttered as heat blossomed in my chest. I blinked several times as my pulse quickened. But I remained silent.

"We're registering fear, General," the doctor reported. "Pain consistent with level one."

Harris nodded. "Excellent." He returned his attention to me. "That was just a little *buzz*, Miss Huang. Quick and easy. But we can sustain that charge for as long as we need to. I'd hate to zap you longer than needed, my dear. So let's answer the questions, yes? Or next time, the charge will be held for thirty seconds."

Thirty seconds doesn't sound too bad. We can handle thirty seconds, I thought to myself.

I was wrong.

When I refused to answer again, Harris ordered another electrical charge, and thirty seconds felt like an eternity. After only a few seconds of the electricity firing through my veins, I started convulsing. I lost control of my body, shaking and spasming against my bindings. But I refused to yell out. I refused to show weakness.

When the charge finally ended, I panted, desperate for breath. My head lolled against my collar as my muscles struggled to carry the weight of my head.

"Pain consistent with level two thresholds, sir," the doctor reported from the corner.

Oh, holy stars. If that was level two…? How many levels were there?

"Are you ready to cooperate, my dear? Let's try this one more time. What is your name?"

My breathing was still ragged, and I swore my heartbeat was irregular. "June… My name…is June." I struggled for breath, to speak without gasping for it.

"Give me your complete name," he said with a victorious smile.

"June…Huang. Name is…June…Huang."

Harris looked back to the doctor.

"A lie, sir."

What?

The general shook his head in disappointment. "The truth, my dear. Only the truth." He flagged his hand at the doctor, and the whirring sound sang through the room once more. My body jolted from the shock, rattling and writhing against my bindings.

When he asked me a third time for my name, I could hardly speak. But I only gave him the same answer. And then I convulsed again, and again, and again. No matter how many times he asked me my name, I only ever said *June Huang*.

And when I finally lost count…

When I thought for sure smoke had to be rising from my cooked body…

General Harris's cool facade finally broke. "I will only ask you once more, girl. What is your *name*?" he yelled at me. His voice boomed and reverberated off the walls.

Stay strong, Lin. Stay strong, my intuition encouraged.

I mustered everything I had within myself to speak as clearly and coherently as possible. "My name…is June Huang…asshole. And you…can go…to hell."

"So be it," he sneered. He flagged his hand, and the room vibrated from the electrical energy blasting through the system.

I convulsed.

I writhed.

I withered.

And I just couldn't help it…

I screamed.

It was only thirty seconds.

But it felt like it lasted an eternity.

And I think I might have died.

***

I woke up to find myself on the floor of my cell, and everything inside of me felt *singed*. And I hurt. I hurt so bad…so much worse than any broken bone, split lip, and bruise I had ever received before. Every nerve inside of me felt like it was withering…dying.

But you made it, Lin. You didn't break. My conscience spoke softly, tenderly. And suddenly, she took shape.

"Edith?" I could barely hear my voice. It cracked and rasped as it flowed through my scorched vocal cords. I saw my little sister, clear as day, with the same sleek black hair, almond-shaped eyes, and porcelain skin as me. Wearing the same blue jeans, white shirt, and dark brown leather jacket and matching boots as the last time I saw her—the day I left home.

She smiled at me. *You made it, Liddy. And I'm so proud of you.*

Tears prickled my eyes. *It hurts so bad, little sis. It hurts so much.*

I could see her in my mind's eye, crouching beside me. Could almost feel her stroking my hair. *I know it hurts, but you're stronger than this. You've always been stronger than anything*, she said with an encouraging smile.

I tried to shake my head but couldn't. My body hardly responded to my commands. "I…I don't think…I'm strong…enough…for this."

You are *strong enough. And I'm going to be with you.* Edith laid down on the floor beside me, tucking her hands under her head. *Go to sleep, Lin. Just sleep.*

That's what I did. I slept.

16: Dangerous Thoughts

I shivered on the stone. Sensations other than pain were slowly coming back, and I realized I was cold. When my eyes opened, Edith was gone. I tried to move, but everything was sore. My muscles responded, though, which was a good sign.

I was still wearing the stupid red dress May had given me, but it was looking less like a dress and more like rags. The lace was torn in several places. My left strap had snapped, and the color had faded into burnt crimson—dirty and grimy. My toes were numb. Never did I ever think that I would crave my stupid heels. I trembled, wishing I had my shoes again.

A muted buzz sounded, startling me. I looked up at the door as the metal ground against itself, and the lock slid back.

Oh no…not again. Please, not again. I tried to scramble to my feet, but I couldn't. So I settled for crawling on the floor, my knees aching against the harsh stone. Huddled in a corner, I curled myself up as the door swung open, and the shadows of two officers blocked out the light in the hallway.

"Prisoner JH4456." Male. Older. Mature.

I swallowed, unsure if he was asking me or merely confirming who I was to the other officer. I refused to answer them. I turned my face, closing my eyes. I was afraid, but I refused to show fear. I didn't know if I could withstand another round of interrogation, but I had to try. I couldn't *break*.

"You understand what you're supposed to do?" the same voice asked.

"Yes." Male. Younger.

"Let me know when you're finished." Shuffling of boots on stone. Grinding metal and the door closing. *Click* and *clack* of the lock sliding into place.

I swallowed.

"I need you to stand." His voice was smooth…deep…rich.

I shivered, but I refused to respond. I tucked my chin to my chest. *Don't break. Whatever he does to you, stay strong.*

"Don't make this harder than it has to be." Different. Accented. *Familiar.* "Por favor…stand."

My eyes shot open. My heart backfired at the familiar purr of those sensuous foreign words. "English." I turned to face the officer. "Speak English."

He looked just as beautiful as I remembered. Black glossy locks of hair framing eyes that looked like precious stones of onyx. Powerful jaw, tall, broad shoulders, and dressed in his new navy-blue REG uniform. The only difference was that the look he gave me no longer held the familiar smug smile or hungry eyes. It was all replaced by a scowl that needled my heart.

"Please," he said. "It means *please*."

Oh my stars, it hurt to look at him. Somehow, in a span of mere days, I went from hating this man to wanting him. From seeing him as all bad to recognizing that good lived within him.

But I hurt him.

I was going to kill him.

And he caught me red-handed.

"Javier—"

"Officer de la Puente," he corrected me, sharp like Honor's edge. "Stand," he ordered.

As if it was even possible, his correction stung fiercer than the volts of electricity that had run through me earlier. I nodded. Gripping the wall, I forced myself to stand, my legs protesting. My fingers dug into the stone walls of my cell, seeking leverage. Once I stood, I locked my knees in place.

His brows knitted together, twitching, softening, then tensing once more. "I'm supposed to clean you, and then dress you in these," he said, holding up gray linen in his hands. "I…" he faltered. Looked away to the corner of the room before bringing his gaze back to me. "I can let you do it yourself, if you prefer?"

My breath caught. "You," my voice rasped. I had to stop and clear it a few times to smooth it out. Finally, I could speak more like myself. "You would do that?"

A flicker through his eyes. A shift of emotion through the schooled expression on his face. "Contrary to what you think of me, Miss Huang, not all Telvians are *evil* and deserving of the end of your blades."

I grimaced. "I didn't mean it like—"

"I don't care what you meant," he shot out. "Can you do it yourself, or do I need to do it for you?"

"I-I can do it."

"Good." It was the crack of a whip. How could one benign word sound so harsh? He tossed the clothing at my feet. "This bucket has water and a sponge," he explained as he stepped forward and placed it a yard away from me, along with something that looked like a towel. He backed away, putting plenty of distance between us.

I didn't move.

"If—" From this distance and with the poor lighting, it was hard to tell, but it seemed he was warring with something. He blew out a breath. "If I turn around, should I be concerned que me vas a matar?" He closed his eyes, shaking his head lightly, and then translated, "I mean, if I turn around, should I be concerned that you'll try to kill me?"

A stab to the chest. "No," I said honestly. Not only was I lacking strength, but I found I had no desire to hurt this man…not anymore.

He shook his head, muttering to himself as he turned around. "Estoy loco. Esta muchacha me eva matar, y aquí estoy yo como un tonto, dándole mi espalda. Mi padre se está rodando en su tumba."

I stumbled for the bucket, hesitated for a moment, but then quickly stripped off my dress. "Do I even want to know what you're saying?"

He laughed, cold and heartless. "I'm saying that I'm insane to give you my back when I have no doubt you were going to murder me that night. My father's rolling in his grave right now."

I said nothing. Only a coward would tell him he was wrong. I had more dignity than that. I focused on the task at hand, diving my hand into the bucket for the sponge. Holy crap, the water was cold. It had to be near freezing.

He snickered again. "At least you have the decency not to deny it."

I raised the sponge and hissed at the sting of icy water against my skin. "It wasn't personal," I said as my breath left my lungs with a shiver. "Damn, this is cold," I muttered to myself.

"It's not supposed to be pleasant."

"Mission accomplished."

He scoffed, but it was warmer. Familiar.

I worked quickly, wiping down the most sensitive parts of me. It was definitely strange to be naked with Javier de la Puente only yards away from me, and the simple thought sent a pump of heat through my chest.

"Why me?" he asked after a moment.

My hand froze, sponge over my breast. "What do you mean?" I continued scrubbing my chest.

His head shifted, and I saw his cheek…the profile of his nose and mouth. And suddenly, I was reminded of their shape.

Of how they looked when they parted.

Of how they felt pressed against mine.

Of how his breath filled my lungs.

Of how his tongue tasted gliding along my lip.

"Why were you going to kill me?"

The memory of lustful kisses was shattered, replaced by the look of hurt on his face when he found my dagger. I grimaced, my heart aching with the sound of his voice. What a question… How do I explain that the only reason he was ordered to die was because he was paying for his uncle's crimes?

And then it hit me…

Were the Dissenters no better than the Telvians? I was being ordered to assassinate a man simply because of his last name, not because of anything he had ever done.

I hated him for it…for that simple surname, *de la Puente*.

I hated him for the blood he carried in his veins and pumped through his heart. For the associations he had, not because he had ever done anything to deserve it.

All expression dropped from my face, and a shudder that had nothing to do with icy water rattled me to my core. Because I realized at that moment that I hated Javier de la Puente because I was *told* to hate him. Knowing nothing about who he was, I was *taught* to hate, and so I did.

My throat closed up. How did it get so twisted? When did the rug get pulled from under my feet and the world turned upside down?

"Está bien…it's fine. You don't have to tell me why." His head shifted again, his profile disappearing.

We stayed silent as I finished quickly, and then got dressed. When I was done, I stepped away from the bucket, back towards the wall.

"Finished," I muttered.

He turned around, eyeing me as though he was studying me. Then he stepped forward and grabbed the bucket.

"Do I get shoes? I can't feel my toes."

He blinked, eyes flickering as he frowned. "No."

"Oh." I bent over and grabbed my blanket, draping it around my shoulders. "Thank you."

His jaw clenched, but he gave me a nod. After that, Javier let the jailer outside the door know he was done through a little window I hadn't noticed previously. It opened from the outside and closed once he handed Javier a paper cup and a bottle.

He faced me. "Your nourishment pill and water," he explained as he placed them on the floor, and then grabbed the bucket and discarded linen, including my dress. "Hasta luego, Miss Huang," he said, words falling flat. Then he was gone.

I stood there for what felt like an eternity, wrestling with my thoughts. What if everything I was fighting for was wrong? What if things weren't as clear cut as I had always been trained to believe? What if…what if the Dissenters were making a mistake?

That's a dangerous line of thinking, Lin. Can you really afford to think that way when tomorrow they're going to strap you to that chair again? It was Edith, stepping out of the shadows of my cell with her arms crossed.

My face crumpled. My chest tightened. "No."

17: A Light in the Dark

Two more days passed just like that one. I would be dragged to Interrogation Room 4, strapped to that chair, and ordered by General Harris to give him my name.

I didn't.

Then the shocks came. The first one was always the same quick little zap. But after that, they got progressively longer and more intense. By the second day, Harris was ordering level 4, and I was screaming every single time the volts shot through my system. But I never told him my damn name…and he was pissed. He ordered a level 5 shock, and I couldn't fight it. I passed out only ten seconds in, though it felt like an hour of convulsing in the chair.

Each time I fell unconscious, I would wake up in my cell on the floor. Edith would lie with me, stroking my hair, whispering how proud she was of me. I missed her. I missed my parents. I missed my friends. I missed my freedom.

You'll see us all again soon, she whispered to me. *You just have to stay strong, Lin. You can't break.*

"Okay," I said, pushing through a muffled cry. Tears blurred my vision. "I'll try. I'll keep trying."

On the third day, when the door opened, I had steeled myself for the next wave of interrogation. But the person who stepped through my door was not who I expected.

"Miss Huang?"

I was huddled in the corner, wrapped in my stupid blanket. *That voice… I know that voice.* I looked up. "Chase?"

He stepped into the room, two officers flanking him. "Good morning, Miss Huang. I'm here to conduct another health assessment." Shakily, I got to my feet. He stepped toward me, bag in hand, placing as much distance between him and the jailers as possible. "How are you?" he whispered as he looked inside my ear with an otoscope.

"I think you can guess."

He looked at my other ear. "I'm sorry, June." He placed both hands on my throat, making little circles and kneading my skin. "I'm trying to understand their rotation schedule for the staff. It's complicated. I think they do it on purpose to make it hard for a breakout."

"Damn Telvians," I groused.

He leaned down, dropping the otoscope in his bag and pulled out a stethoscope instead. He placed the end against my chest and began listening to my heart. "You're holding up well. That's good."

I snorted. "I'd hate to know what holding up *bad* looks like."

He smirked, shifting the end piece to hear my lungs. "I found May."

"You did?" I said just a hair too loudly.

"Shh," Chase chastised.

I glimpsed over his shoulder. The guards watched us for a moment and then went back to muttering to each other. I looked back at him and nodded.

"There's another level of inmates below us. She's there." He moved the end piece to my back, and then ordered me to take several breaths. I did. Then he whispered again, "My colleague has her on her roster. I'll try to keep an eye on her for you."

I closed my eyes, the corner of my lips tugging for a smile I couldn't let them have. May was alive, and Chase was going to see how he could help her. Thank the stars for him. He was a good man. If he wasn't already spoken for, I'd seriously consider signing up and offering myself as tribute.

"I have to feel under your arms, okay?" he said loud enough for the guards to hear. He rubbed his hands together hard and fast. "They're cold," he warned.

"Okay."

Then he was pressing into my armpits, kneading me as his hands shifted downwards. Whispering, he said, "I don't have a plan yet, but I'm going to keep trying, okay?"

I nodded. He dropped the stethoscope into his bag and pulled out a syringe.

"What's that?" Alarm bells sounded in my head.

He winked. "Miss Huang, I'm giving you an injection of Everclear."

I arched a brow at him.

He lowered his voice, quickly mouthing, "Saline."

I blew out a quiet breath of relief, but quickly placed a look of fear on my face. "What is it?"

Chase grabbed my arm and pushed up the gray long sleeve, exposing the sensitive skin that shielded my veins. "It's part of Stage 2 of the Interrogation Program. You don't need to worry about it. It just helps keep you healthy." Then he dropped his voice again. "This shit keeps you conscious so they can increase the shock levels and keep you awake longer. Makes it harder for people to resist telling the truth."

Yish! No thank you.

The needle pierced my skin, and Chase slowly pushed down on the plunger. "I swapped yours out for saline," he explained as he slowly pulled out the needle and then pressed a cotton ball to the spot. "Lean into the pain, June. When you pass out, you're done for the day. Lean in and let your consciousness go."

I nodded, replacing his fingers with mine over the cotton. Chase capped the needle, stored it, and then brought out a bandaid. "It looks like I check on you every three to four days, okay? I'll be back."

"Thank you," I whispered as he took the cotton ball and replaced it with the bandaid.

He collected his bag. "Stay strong." Louder he said, "I'm finished," and then he left. I was once again alone with nothing but my thoughts.

★★★

Later that day, they came for me. When my cell door opened, I was huddled in my corner, trying to stay warm. In marched Officer Ugly followed by familiar onyx eyes.

"Miss Huang, por favor, párate." Without a second's pause, he translated, "Please stand."

With a deep breath, I rose to my bare feet.

"Turn around," Ugly snapped at me.

I did, but I glanced over my shoulder to watch as Ugly grabbed harshly at my wrists, twisting them more than necessary. I bit down, refusing to show pain.

"¿Es necesario hacerlo así?" There was a sharpness to Javier's tone.

Ugly paused, still holding my wrist twisted so much that I had to dip my shoulder to find some relief from the unnatural angle. "*What?*" he groused.

"Is it necessary to do it like that?" Javier snapped back. I heard it...annoyance, frustration, and...something else.

Ugly said nothing, but he twisted my wrist just a hair more, causing my shoulder to dip further. "Why does it matter?" he grated out. It was definitely a rhetorical question.

"Dame eso." The words came out like an order. I watched from my limited peripheral vision as Javier shoved the other officer. My wrists were let go, and I sighed as I straightened my posture.

"What's your *problem*, man?"

Warm hands took my wrist—soft, gentle, light.

"You're not royalty down here, de la Puente. I don't take orders from *you*." Ugly was raising his voice, almost shouting.

The hands were gone from my wrist, but I didn't dare turn around. I glimpsed over my shoulder again and watched as Javier got right into Ugly's face. "Don't test me, Cabrera. I fucking kicked your ass yesterday, didn't I? I'll do it again."

Edith's voice sang in my head. *I like this one, Lin. He's feisty.*

I twisted at the waist to get a better view, ignoring Edith.

Cabrera brought his face so close to Javier's, their noses almost touched. Through gritted teeth, he spat out, "I'm going to report you, asshole—"

Javier's hands snapped out, grabbing Ugly by the collar of his shirt and yanked him forward. "Do it. I *dare* you." The words came out slow and menacing, and all the color drained from Cabrera's face. After a few seconds, he swallowed, and his eyes shifted away. "That's what I thought." Javier shoved him back, letting go of his collar.

Ugly stumbled a step or two before he regained his footing. He glared at Javier, the two simply staring each other down. Pulling on his shirt to straighten his uniform, Cabrera finally said, "I hope she shanks your ass, de la Puente." He rolled his shoulders and cracked his neck. "I'll wait outside." Then he walked out the door.

Silence.

All I had was Javier's back—delicious broad shoulders that rolled as he straightened himself. He began to turn, and I quickly whipped back around to face the wall. I heard the shuffling of boots, and then I felt the warmth of his hands as they took my wrist once more.

So gentle…if I closed my eyes, I could pretend it was a caress if I wanted to.

You did, Edith acknowledged. *And I don't blame you either*, she added.

"Did he hurt you?" he asked quietly, slowly grabbing my other wrist.

I shook my head. "No."

I felt the binders snap around one wrist, and then the other. "I'm sorry."

My stomach clenched. "Why? You didn't do anything."

He didn't answer. "Turn around."

I did as I was told, hands now restrained behind my back. That schooled blank face was in place, and I realized I missed his smug smile and laughing eyes. How funny that back then I wanted nothing more than to smack them off his face…and now I craved them.

His gaze shifted to the ground as his jaw ticked. He was trying to figure something out. I could just see his mind twisting and turning with his internal struggle. I wanted to know. I wanted to peer into his mind, hear his thoughts, feel the emotions I knew were inside him.

You like him, don't you? Edith came out of the shadows once more, stepping forward to stand just behind him, and it was as though time stopped. Everything froze. She folded her arms across her chest.

I… I don't know. It was the truth. I truly didn't know. All I knew was that he fascinated me. He pulled out the most interesting combination of emotions from the depths of my soul. He made me feel hot and thrilled and dangerous and exhilarated.

Yes, you do. My sister took slow steps, walking around us with a knowing smile that said she saw way more than what was being depicted. *You know exactly how you feel, Liddy. You're just afraid to admit it.*

I pinched my brows, chewing on my bottom lip. *It doesn't matter what I feel, little sis. Last I checked, he's about to walk me into another torture session. Not exactly romantic, now is it?*

She snorted. *I feel like there's an entire community of people who would largely disagree with you.*

I smiled. Shifted my gaze to Javier's frozen face. He really was beautiful. Exotic. Dark and dangerous, and yet...*comforting*. I looked at my sister. *Will you stay with me?*

Edith's eyes glimmered as she offered me a soothing smile. *I'm with you, Lin. Just like when we were kids...I'm with you.*

"June."

I blinked, my mind snapping back into reality. "What?"

Javier was standing in front of me, hands holding my face, eyes boring into mine. "¿Estás bien? Are you okay?"

I blinked several more times, surprised to find him cradling my face. It was such a sweet and tender gesture...as though he cared. I took a deep breath. "Yeah," I finally managed, but he seemed unconvinced.

His eyes searched mine, worry on his brow. "Are you sure? It was like you weren't here, like you were spaced out?"

My lips parted. "I guess I..." My words dropped off as my gaze met his. I saw the flicker in his obsidian eyes. Felt the heat of his body so close to mine. And that mouth...those lips, twisted in a frown.

It clicked.

Does he...care? I thought to myself. "I'm sorry," I muttered. "I didn't mean to worry you."

His eyes widened for a heartbeat as his lips parted. It happened quickly, but I saw it. I saw the shock—the *surprise*—that flashed across his gorgeous features. Then he closed his mouth, stepping away as all emotion was wiped clean from his face. He cleared his throat. "Exit first," he said. "I'll follow behind." But he didn't correct me. He didn't *deny* it.

Javier de la Puente *worried*, which meant that...

Javier de la Puente *cared*.

If he cares, then he might help, Edith whispered in the corner of my mind. *There's hope, Lin. He just might be your ticket out of here.*

18: Find the Black

General Harris stood with his hands behind his back as he always did. "You have all the power here, my dear. All you have to do is tell me your name. That's it. Tell me your name, and I'll pull you out of that chair."

My traitorous heart thundered in my chest. I knew what was coming. I knew how it would feel as the electricity traveled through my blood. I inhaled, preparing myself for the inevitable.

Remember what Chase said. Lean into the pain. My eyes shifted to Edith standing by the wall, right next to Javier. His face was expressionless.

"Now, tell me your real name."

I gritted my teeth, remaining silent.

Harris tsked, shaking his head, and then waved his hand at the doctor in the corner. The whirring sound filled the room, and then I was shocked. But it was so much worse than before. My body rattled against my bindings, and my insides felt like they were blowing up like a balloon.

Five seconds…

Ten seconds…

Fifteen seconds…

A scream erupted from me, shrill and piercing.

Twenty seconds…

And then it stopped. My body slackened against my restraints, the collar digging into my neck. I panted, my heart beating with an irregular rhythm.

"Your name. What is your real name?" Harris ordered forcefully.

My eyes fluttered. "June…Huang."

The general waved again. The whirring kicked up, and then I was shuddering in my chair once more, screaming at the top of my lungs.

Ten seconds...

Twenty seconds...

Thirty seconds...

It all stopped, and my head flopped against the collar. I tried to lift it, but my muscles struggled to respond.

"What are we at?" Harris asked the doctor.

"Level 5, sir."

"Increase to six."

Fear pooled in my gut, twisting my intestines. My eyes searched past the general...searched for my sister.

I'm here, Lin. Stay strong. Look for the black, she coached, stepping forward to stand by Harris. I could do that. Find the edge of my consciousness and fade into the black.

"What is your *name*!" It was no longer a question but a yelled command.

I panted, my heart's irregular rhythm causing waves of nausea. I lifted my eyes because I couldn't hold up my head and saw my sister. Then my vision shifted focus, and I saw *him*. Those black eyes gazed right at me, face twisted in a scowl. But something about those eyes whispered. I only wish I knew what they said.

"I'm...June Huang...asshole. Go. To. *Hell*."

Harris growled, waving his hand. The whirring kicked up once more, and the world flashed into stars as electricity pulsed through me. A guttural scream erupted from my lungs once more.

"Increase to seven!"

Find the black, Lin! Edith shouted at me, but I couldn't see her face. The whirring intensified, and my entire body burned as I writhed against my bounds. *Find the black now!*

And then I was gone, finally diving into the darkness that was the black.

★★★

I shivered, the cold slowly coming into my awareness. When my eyes opened, I wasn't sprawled in the middle of the floor. I was in my corner, with my body curled up on top of my moth-eaten blanket. I blinked, my cell slowly coming into focus.

Something rough brushed against my cheek.

A blanket...I had a second blanket covering me. This one wool—thicker, warmer than the other. I huddled under it, relishing the small kindness.

You did wonderfully, Liddy. My eyes searched, and I found her. Edith stepped out of the shadows and came to sit next to me, her raven black hair falling forward.

What happened?

You went unconscious, she said, stating the obvious.

Where did the second blanket come from?

She opened her mouth to answer, but the sound of metal grinding caused her to look at the door. Then she was gone, and I shifted my gaze to the steel door as it swung open. The profile of an officer filled the doorway, and I watched as they stepped inside, the door closing behind them.

"Miss Huang?" Male. Smooth. Rich.

I tried to sit up. The profile shifted and then stepped forward. Javier came into focus.

"Do you need help?" There was a strain in his voice, and he didn't wait for me to answer. He crouched down and took hold of my arm while his other hand went to my side, slowly righting me so I could sit.

I panted, resting my head against the wall. "Thank you."

His hands lingered for a moment, and then finally let go. "De nada."

"English..." I tried offering him a smile. I failed.

"It means you're welcome," he said softly with a half-hearted smirk.

I swallowed, my mouth dry and aching for water. "I'm so thirsty."

He pulled on a strap across his chest, lifted it over his head, and swung forward a bag I hadn't noticed. Reaching into it, he pulled out a bottle of water. "Here."

I gaped at him, surprised by the kind gesture, but I grabbed the bottle, opened it, and guzzled it.

"Whoa! Esperate," he said as he grabbed my wrists, pulling them away gently. "Drink slowly or you'll upset your stomach. I could only find one extra blanket, so if you ruin this one, you'll be stuck without it."

I stilled, my shoulders dropping at his words. "*You* brought me the blanket?" There was no way. I watched him, searching for any hint of a lie. Saw as his face shifted—lashes splayed over his cheeks, lips frowned. Then he took a deep breath and nodded. My heart softened and then puddled into nothing in my chest. "Why?"

"You were shivering." His voice was so soft, so...*ached*. "Y después de lo que vi..." he faltered, turning his head to stare into the darkness.

He was still holding my wrists, and even though I wanted another drink, I didn't dare move—too afraid that he would let me go. I spoke instead.

"I don't understand what you said."

Slowly, he faced me again, and his black eyes showed me sorrow...and pain. "Never mind... How are you feeling?" He let me go, and instantly I missed his warmth.

"Not great," I resolved, lifting the bottle to my lips and sipping.

He snickered. "I can only imagine."

Silence fell between us, and I drank more of the water, enjoying the way it soothed my raw throat.

"Why won't you tell him your name?"

I backwashed into my bottle as I choked. "What?"

He shrugged. "It's a simple question, June."

I rubbed my lips. How do you explain to someone like him why you would rather face torture than give up something so personal—so *sacred*—as your name?

I sighed. "Because I..." I hesitated, the words hanging on my tongue. But after a heartbeat, I tipped my chin to my chest. "I don't want him to think he can break me." It was an honest answer. I lifted my eyes and caught as he looked at me. A steady gaze...as though he was slowly peeling the layers back of who I was.

Then he nodded. "I can respect that."

Warmth bloomed inside me, and the corners of my lips tugged, wanting to smile. I wish I could say that I thought it through, but I didn't. And when the words left my lips, I was just as surprised to hear them as he was. "Liddy. My name's Liddy Le."

The obsidian eyes glowed with a light that seemed to brew from his soul.

"But everyone calls me Lin."

Silence. Several breaths. Several heartbeats. And then… "Why would you tell me?"

My heart took a plunge like a dove diving through the air. I whispered, "Because I have faith."

19: Falling is Scary

The following day, I was dragged out again by Officer Cabrera and some woman I didn't recognize. Harris started at Level 6, but only got through three rounds before I found the black and disappeared into unconsciousness. When I woke up, I was sprawled on my stomach in the middle of my room once more.

Eventually, I crawled to my corner and replayed every memory I had of Javier. From the first day I met him at the Academy, down to the moment his face broke at the recognition of my words: *I have faith.* That was the most interesting part...

I did.

I didn't know why, and I didn't know when it happened.

Maybe it was the day he saved me from Tim Harris and his goons.

Maybe it was when he told me why he continued to speak a language long forgotten by most others.

Maybe it was when he let me go, knowing full well what I was and assuming too accurately what I had been tasked to do.

Or maybe—just maybe—it was the simple fact that he had kept my identity a secret. Because even though twenty-four hours had passed since I told Javier my name, General Harris still ached to know who I was.

Yes. Something deep inside of me had shifted, and I realized I trusted Javier de la Puente. I trusted him with my truth. I trusted he wouldn't betray me. I trusted him with my life.

I had faith.

I could only hope I didn't come to regret it.

***

The door opened, and I watched as Chase entered. The female jailer stood by the door as he came towards me.

"I'm here to conduct another health assessment, Miss Huang." He dropped the bag and quickly started looking in my ears. "Are you okay?" he whispered.

"As okay as I can be."

He nodded, kneading my throat. "Harris is ordering another dose of Everclear. He says you're passing out too fast in the interrogation process." He smiled defiantly.

I suppressed a grin. "Any news on May?"

He grimaced, grabbing his stethoscope from his bag. "Yeah. She's not doing as well as you are. She's not getting saline, and the Everclear is keeping her conscious for too long."

She's going to crack, Lin, Edith said, materializing from the shadows. *She needs to get out of here, or she's going to end up telling them everything.*

I know. "Is there any hope of breaking us out?"

Chase instructed me to breathe, listening to my lungs. "I'm trying, June. I swear, but none of the schedules make sense. The rotation seems almost random, and if I can't figure it out, I don't know that I can get you both out."

I blew out a breath, feeling the end piece of his stethoscope travel under the hem of my shirt at my back and stopping over my lungs.

"I need to talk to one of the officers…see if I can get one of them to talk and explain the schedule to me." He dropped the stethoscope into his bag.

"Keep trying."

He nodded. "Arms out."

I held my arms out perpendicular to my legs. Chase's hands kneaded under my arms and then traveled down my sides.

"I found Sally."

My eyes widened. "Is she okay?"

He nodded. "She's fine. Happy with her new career. But she's worried about you."

"Did you tell her I'm here?"

He shook his head. "No. I didn't want to risk her or myself any more than necessary." He reached down into his bag.

That made sense. The less Sally knew, the better. Poor Chase was already in this too deep. "I'm sorry, Chase."

He gave me a half smile. "What are friends for, right?" Out loud, he ordered, "Give me your arm." I offered it to him and watched as he took a syringe from his bag and pierced my skin with the needle.

"I'll be back in a few days, okay?" He pulled out the needle, capped it, and then stored it in his bag.

"I owe you," I whispered.

"Stay alive and I'll consider the debt repaid." He flashed me one of his smug, characteristic smirks that made most girls drop to their knees at the Academy. All I could do was smile. He grabbed his bag, announcing he was done, and then I was left alone once more.

★★★

"Tell me your name!" He didn't even wait to see if I would answer. The whirring kicked on and I convulsed, my head whipping furiously.

Twenty seconds…

Thirty seconds…

Forty seconds…

"Level 9!" General Harris yelled.

"But, sir, it hasn't been—"

"Nine!" he roared.

I thrashed uncontrollably, desperately looking for the black as the whirring rose to a high-pitched squeal.

"General, *stop*!" Male. Smooth. Rich. Beautiful. "You're going to kill her!"

Fifty-five…

Sixty seconds…

It stopped, and I collapsed against my restraints, panting like a dog in the summer. My heart's irregular rhythm made me feel like it was going to combust at any moment.

Find the black, Lin. Edith was on the platform, crouched on her knees in front of me. *Look for it. Lean into the pain.*

"When I want your input, Officer de la Puente, I'll ask for it." The general turned to face my direction. But I wasn't looking at him. My eyes were set on Javier, who looked like he was about to crack a molar with the ferocity of his sneer.

"I'm going to ask one final time, my dear, and then you'll regret you were ever even born. What is your *name*?"

I didn't think I could answer him even if I wanted to. But I had no desire to give this man *anything*. Silence suited me just fine.

He growled—a deep, menacing rumble that rattled my very core. "So be it." He flagged the doctor. The machine sang to life.

Edith grabbed my hand, screaming, *Find the black!*

Just as the electricity ignited my veins, I found the end of my consciousness, and dove off the edge.

★★★

I sobbed, gripping my skinned knee. "I don't want to bike anymore," I cried. I had fallen off, a tumble that left my leg bloody and badly scraped. "I'm scared."

Edith stood next to me, hand on her hip as she stared at me on the asphalt. She was missing her two front teeth. One was natural. But once she figured out money was involved, she paid a boy at school to punch her and knock out the second one. Her hot pink helmet had a flaming blue mohawk. She swore it made her look cool. I thought it made her look like a crazed rooster.

"Bikes aren't scary, Lin. Falling is scary."

"Fine," I scowled. "Then I'm scared of falling."

"Then just don't fall, duh," she drawled.

I glared at her. "I'm not falling on purpose, Edith."

"Yes, you are," she argued back.

"No, I'm not!"

"Sure you are. Because you're scared of it, you make yourself fall. Stop being scared of it, and then it won't happen," she reasoned.

I rolled my eyes. "That doesn't make any sense—"

"Yeah, it does. Don't be afraid, and then you won't fall. That's when you'll learn how to fly."

***

The chill stirred once again in my bones, and just like before, I felt the rough texture of one blanket under one cheek, and another cuddling the other. Shuffling greeted my ears, and my eyes fluttered open. The room was blurry at first, but slowly came into focus.

Someone was with me.

He paced back and forth in my cell. He ran his hands through his hair, rubbed the back of his neck for a moment, and then dropped them to his side, only to be shoved into his hair again a moment later. Back and forth, back and forth. I heard him blow out a breath. I listened as he muttered to himself with those foreign words I wished so badly I understood.

Then he'd stop, one arm folded across his midsection, propping up the elbow of the other as his fist rested against his jaw. He was anxious energy—hot and heavy. And somehow, he looked more breathtaking than ever.

"What's wrong?" My voice was hoarse and raspy. I sounded like a freaking smoker.

He startled. "Liddy?" He closed the distance and dropped to the floor in front of me. "Gracias a dios…you're all right."

"I think *all right* is a bit strong for what I am right now." I tried to sit up, but I just couldn't. My muscles struggled to respond.

He muttered under his breath as he reached to help me sit up. "I thought you were dead. When he ordered that last round, I thought for sure he killed you."

Slowly, gently, tenderly, Javier tucked a strand of my hair behind my ear. Then his thumb lingered, stroking my cheek. Silence fell between us, and all I could do was look into his black eyes. I loved the way they took in every square inch of me. Loved the way it felt to be touched by him, to be so close that I could smell the lavender and cedar coming off his skin.

"I don't know how much more you're going to be able to take of this," he whispered. One heartbeat, two heartbeats… His gaze hardened. "Just tell him what he wants to know. Tell him and then it'll be done."

I shook my head weakly. "I can't... I swore an oath, and I refuse to bring dishonor to my family."

His brows drew forward in a pained V as he tucked his chin to his chest. I smiled. The small gesture...it was confirmation of what I already knew. That Javier cared about me. How or why, I didn't know, but he absolutely *cared*.

Using everything I had in me, I lifted my hand and took his. "Thank you," I whispered.

His fingers folded around mine. "I'm supposed to clean you up again." He looked over his shoulder and motioned with his head at the bucket and folded linen. "Can you do it yourself?"

"I'll try," I muttered. Every word took so much effort. I *hated* it.

He stood, letting go of me, and brought everything to my corner. Then he took several steps back and turned around.

I stared at the bucket, noticing delicate tendrils of steam curling from the water. *It can't be.* "Is it...*warm*?"

"Yes." Soft. Gentle. Tender. Just one word, and I could almost hear every word begging to be spoken after.

Yes, because I care.

Warmth bloomed like a meadow blossoming in the sun. "I...I don't even know what to say."

I saw his head turn, revealing the profile of his face, lips tugged into a smile. "It's been sitting for a while, so take advantage before it cools too much."

I tried. I started by trying to pull an arm out of my sleeve, but the effort caused me to huff and pant, exhausted without accomplishing anything. I tried again...

Failure.

Then I changed tactics and went for the hem of my shirt instead.

Failure again.

I tried to take off the other sleeve and—

I collapsed against the wall with fatigue.

My head lolled back against the stone as I closed my eyes and almost cried from the frustration. "I can't. It's too hard. My body just won't cooperate." And then I *did* cry.

One tear softly fell down the curve of my cheek. Then another... I was weak, and weakness meant doom lingered in my future. Fear curled inside me. What would happen tomorrow? Or the day after that? How long did I actually think I could withstand minimal nutrition, minimal hydration, and being electrified day after day after day?

Nobody.

Nobody could do this. *Nobody* could survive this.

I'm breaking…

Fingers brushed my cheek, and the soothing smell of lavender filled my senses. "Shh…estás bien, mi vida. It's okay."

I sniffed. "I want a bath so bad." Another tear rolled down. "I feel so…*inhuman*. But everything hurts." I wasn't used to this. I wasn't used to being unable to care for myself, unable to pick up a freaking sponge. "I'm going to die here, aren't I?" It wasn't a real question…it was a realization. Acceptance of the inevitable. I was already walking on the path toward my death, I was just too delusional to see it. And Javier…well, at least he had the decency not to lie to me.

I respected him for that.

His thumb brushed away another tear and then swooped to tuck another strand of my hair behind my ear. "Te puedo ayudar, si quieres… If you really *need* this, I—" he faltered, closing his eyes and swallowing before opening them once more. "I can help you…but only if you want me to."

My eyes widened as my body pressed itself against the wall.

He lifted his hands, palms out. "Only if you want, Liddy. I'm not trying to force myself on you. Te lo prometo…I promise," he translated.

I was a kaleidoscope of emotions. My morale was caving, and something so simple as hot water on my skin could help scrub away the depression slowly breaking me. But the version of me that was Liddy from the Academy was five seconds away from slapping him for even suggesting it. Because *she* was afraid. Afraid of what saying yes *meant*. Afraid of what saying yes might *lead* to.

But the present Liddy—the Liddy that kissed him and remembered how his voice sounded when he challenged General Harris—*that* Liddy…she trusted him. She trusted he would respect her limits and not take advantage of her when she was utterly defenseless and unable to care for herself. And *that* Liddy needed a ray of hope. She needed *faith*.

I looked at him, my heart beating as though I was about to reveal my biggest, darkest truth. "You promise?"

The lines of Javier's face were nothing but strokes of tenderness and affection. A look that left me falling apart, crumbling into nothing. "Sí, mi vida. With my life."

20: Snapped

The moment I agreed was the second my heart began pattering to a rhythm I hardly recognized. He settled close to me, placing the basin beside us, along with the folded fresh linens ready to replace my soiled clothing. He lifted his hands, fingers curling back as he hesitated, and all I could do was take a deep breath to steady my achy heart.

With ginger movements, Javier reached for the hem of my shirt and slowly drew it up. Cool, crisp air greeted my abdomen, and then traveled up to my chest. He guided one arm out of the sleeve, then the other, and then lifted the shirt over my head. I shivered. I longed to fold my arms across my chest. Instinct told me that's what I needed to do, but I couldn't lift my arms that high. All I could do was cross them over my stomach and rest them in my lap.

Javier reached for the towel, unfolded it, and then draped it along my back, wrapping it around me, tucking the hem into each one of my hands, offering me the illusion of control. The gesture caused my chest to tighten. I didn't have to read his mind to know he was trying to keep me warm and make me comfortable.

Then he dipped his hand into the basin, pulled out the sponge, and squeezed out the excess water. He cleared his throat softly. "¿Estás lista? Are you ready?"

My heart was pounding. Swallows dove and twirled and danced in my stomach. "Yes."

I watched him swallow, realizing in that moment that he was just as nervous as I was. His hand slipped past the towel, and the hot sponge touched the skin of my sternum. I trembled, closing my eyes at how wonderful the heat felt against my chest.

"Too hot?"

I rested my head back against the wall. "No," I whispered. "It's perfect."

The sponge moved slowly in little circles for a moment, before he drew it out and dunked it back into the bucket. Then it was on my skin again, stroking my collarbone. Eventually, the embarrassment drifted away, and I watched him instead. He studied me carefully, always looking for any signs of discomfort, and he never allowed his gaze to drift to my bare chest for more than a second, trying hard to be respectful. His touch was always tender, each stroke feeling more like I was being caressed by the soft hands of a lover than the touch of a sponge.

It was...*intimate*. So incredibly intimate, and—dare I say it—*loving*. I could hardly speak. The way he bathed me...

The way he softly cleansed away the traces of the last several days...

It was as though my very soul was being washed of my torment.

You like him, Lin. My sister's voice was in my ear.

The sponge traveled down the length of my arm. *I do*, I answered. There was no point in lying to myself.

I heard her chuckle softly. *But you are, sis. You're lying to yourself.*

I shifted my gaze off him, tucking my chin.

You're starting to love him.

My breath hitched at the accusation.

"Perdóname...forgive me. Too rough?" His eyes sought mine, the sponge frozen on my hip.

"No," I managed in a breathless whisper. "It's fine."

The way my heart skipped a beat...

The way my chest twisted into a death grip...

The way my soul vibrated at the mere thought...

Edith was right. She always was.

I was falling in love with Javier de la Puente.

The sponge moved gently over my abs to my other side, and all my stupid heart could do was patter as I realized what was happening to me. My entire body quivered.

"Is it too cold?" His eyes searched mine.

I could barely shake my head. "No."

He pressed his lips together, and I could tell that he was unsure of how to interpret my reactions. He ran his bottom lip through his teeth, and I almost melted right then and there. It was true. It really was *true*. Except, I wasn't *falling* in love…

I think I'm already there, lil' sis. I think I'm already in love with him.

I heard her gentle laugh—the type that comes when you know something someone else didn't. And then she whispered back, *I know.*

Javier dipped the sponge back into the basin, and when he drew it out, it paused right over the hills and valley of my chest. "Um…es tiempo para—" he faltered, clearing his throat.

I smiled, because if my eyes weren't mistaken, Javier de la Puente was blushing.

He licked his lips, taking a deep breath as confident resolve took over him, bringing him back into control. "I'm going to be gentle, mi vida. Unless you prefer me to skip this part?"

A devilish energy consumed my being, and strength I hadn't felt since being locked away inside the earth swelled within me. "No," I replied. "I'm ready."

His eyes darted back and forth, and then he nodded softly. Shifting closer, he brought the warmth of his body next to mine. The sponge dipped back in between the ends of the towel and touched my flushed skin. The heat felt sinfully good against my breasts, and it took everything within me to suppress the moan that begged to escape my lips. His face tipped to the side as he watched his work, watched the sponge glide across my skin.

Soft strokes…

Teasing circles…

Gentle swipes…

I wasn't breathing anymore. My heart wasn't beating anymore. Blood wasn't pumping anymore. I wasn't me. Any. *More.*

I wanted him to watch.

I wanted him to see.

I wanted him to *touch.*

It took every ounce of strength I had left inside of me to lift my hand, and I was relieved when I realized that my strength was returning just as it always had.

My hand took his wrist and halted his movements right over my heart. His onyx eyes drifted to mine, and we both froze, ensnared in each other's gaze.

We didn't speak.

We didn't move.

I don't think either of us even breathed.

I held his wrist in place, my heart thumping hard underneath, as my free hand curled around the roughness of the sponge. I felt the tendons and muscles of his wrist shift underneath my grasp as he let go of it. My eyes never left his as I pulled the sponge away, dropping it beside me.

His lips parted to speak, but I shook my head lightly, silencing him. My heart ached. Want and need pooled low and deep within me, and I knew exactly what I desired. I drew his hand forward and pressed his palm against my flesh.

His eyes flashed. His jaw clenched. And I watched with great satisfaction as Javier's face became a battlefield, fought between his chivalrous moral judgment and the sensuous jaguar that was his primal need.

"Liddy—"

"Lin," I uttered. "Call me Lin."

He paused. One heartbeat. "Lin," he finally breathed out, his whole body rigid as stone. "I'm trying to be good, to keep my promise," he said, voice thick and husky and delicious, making my skin prickle. "And this...*this* doesn't help me."

I smirked. "I've decided promises are made to be broken." I pressed his hand harder against my chest; my heart beating wildly underneath his palm. "*Break it.*"

It was only a second of hesitation. One thunderous heartbeat of a pause. And then the predator that was Javier de la Puente *snapped*.

21: Echoes of Devotion

His lips found mine, tasting just as fresh and minty as I remembered, while his free hand cupped my face with a touch that spoke of tender, quiet longing. Teeth raked my bottom lip, and I answered—parting, welcoming, inviting. The initial contact of his tongue was soft, a delicate, tentative exploration that conveyed a depth of emotion. But I didn't want *delicate*.

I wanted *fire*.
I wanted *heat*.
I wanted *passion*.
I wanted *everything*.

I let go of his wrist, reached out, and dug my fingers into the fabric of his uniform, pulling him closer, begging him to let go of the gossamer thread of control he had left.

"Javier," I whimpered, absolutely loving how his name felt in my mouth. "*Please…*" His body tensed under my hands and all around me, hard as the stone of my prison walls. I nipped his lip, eliciting a guttural groan from inside him.

"Vas a ser mi muerte," he whispered and then translated, "You're going to be the death of me."

"Then let it be so…" I nipped him again, and then it was over. His hand glided around to the small of my back and pulled me forward, lifting me easily and settling me astride his hips. My hands made quick work, undoing each button of his uniform, revealing more and more of his sun-kissed skin and black ink of a tattoo I wanted to explore, but not now. Not when the heat of his body lit me on fire from the inside out.

He kissed me hungrily with no reservations, and our connection deepened with each passing moment as my world of chains and torment faded away with each desperate kiss. His lips moved with purpose, tracing a path along mine that sent shivers down my spine. As passion grew, his hands wandered, exploring the contours of my body with a hunger that mirrored the fire in his obsidian eyes. But he wasn't alone on this one.

Adrenaline was my fuel...

Desire was my strength...

Love was my salvation...

My fingers threaded through his hair, pulling him closer, wanting so much more than what I was being offered. Because if I was going to die in this place, then let me enjoy just one more carnal pleasure...one more wish granted before I succumbed to my doom.

I pulled on his shirt, desperately shoving it off his shoulders. And once again he tensed. Again he halted.

"Lin..."My name fell from his lips like a prayer. "No tengo control, mi vida. I only have so much restraint." I could hear the tension in his voice, could hear him losing the war one fiery touch at a time.

I kissed him, taking his face in my hands as I pulled the very air from his lungs, giving me breath. "Don't deny me. Please...I want this. I *need* this."

The air between us crackled with an undeniable energy, a magnetic force pulling us together.

His nose grazed mine as his eyes lingered on my lips. "Promise me you won't regret this. That tomorrow you won't see me and hate me for what happened. *Promise me.*"

His eyes found mine then, and I saw a world of beauty there. I saw hunger, and honor, and glory, and care, and passion so fierce, I believed that the world would burn if it was ever unleashed. My fingers curled against his face as I cradled him, my forehead resting against his, noses brushing, breaths intermingling. "I promise. There's nothing about you I could ever regret. I *promise.*"

Those obsidian eyes stared into me, boring into my depths, desperately searching for any hesitation. I tipped my head to the side, allowing my lips to graze his as I spoke. "Have faith," I whispered.

He jolted underneath me, and I sensed the moment he caved. Hands stripped away what remained of our clothing, and then they explored my exposed skin. His kisses became more fervent, desire building with an unstoppable intensity, and I was lost in the intoxicating dance of our mouths. I surrendered; I surrendered all of myself to the growing hunger that enveloped us both.

Settling back into his lap, our bodies pressed together as the heat between us rose, beating back the chill in the air. Every kiss stoked the flames of our desire, our breaths mingling in a rhythm that mirrored the pounding of our hearts. And when he found me…when I felt Javier deep inside my core, time stood still.

Cheek pressed against mine, I felt as his lips caressed the shell of my ear. "Te amo, mi vida," he whispered, voice so tender that the purity of it caused me to shiver. And then we danced.

Every move was gentle.

Every shift a declaration of adoration.

Every stroke an echo of devotion.

And we were lost, the outside world fading into insignificance.

And when the hunger between us reached its peak…

When the room pulsed with our shared longing, a symphony of desires and hopes and dreams played out to the shadows of my prison walls…

I released into a shared crescendo of shuddering breaths and whispered promises, trembling against him as his arms folded around me, tucking me into him. I closed my eyes, feeling safe in his arms as I rode each gentle wave, quaking with each satisfying lap, until I grew limp in his embrace.

"Te amo," he repeated in my ear, holding me tight, as though I was the most precious thing.

"What does that mean?" I whispered breathlessly.

He shifted, cradling my face in his hands and drawing my forehead down so that it was pressed against his, noses touching. "It means I love you, Lin. *Te amo* means *I love you*."

★★★

I discovered I loved the feel of my body molded against his. We were wrapped in my blankets, snuggled up in my corner. He had tucked me under his arm, holding me close while my head rested against him. Time was ticking, and even though Javier was the only guard on duty for my cell tonight, every passing second felt like a loss. Morning would soon arrive, and I would have to say goodbye to him.

I watched his chest rise with each breath, and my hand drew up to his sternum, right over the black ink. Shifting, I sat up, turning to better see the tattoo.

Wings.

A pair of black wings spread across his chest with three words in a language I didn't understand inked over them. I muttered them aloud, sounding them out. "Amor vincit omnia." Javier's hand drifted to my face, stroking it, brushing away the stands of my hair that had fallen forward. I whispered the words again before finally looking up into his handsome face. "Is it Spanish?"

He shook his head. "No..."—his thumb grazed my bottom lip—"it's Latin."

I read the words on his skin again. "What does it mean?"

Embers burned in his eyes, remnants of the passion we both so deeply enjoyed just moments ago. "It means, *love conquers all*, mi vida. It always does...always will."

I shuddered under his gaze, loving the way the words sounded coming off his tongue. I took his left hand in mine, lifted it to my lips and brushed his knuckles tenderly with them. Then I turned it over, letting my eyes admire how strong they appeared. My gaze wandered over his palm, landing on the lotus flower rising from rippling waters. "And this one?" I brushed a fingertip over the image. Something about it looked familiar to me. I knew I'd seen it at the Academy, but the familiarity ran deeper than that, as though I had seen it years before somehow. I racked my brain, but I just couldn't pin it. "Does this one mean something?"

He allowed me to touch it, to run my fingers over the blossoming petals. "I don't know if it means anything to anyone, but I know what it means to me."

I looked up at him. Waited. But his eyes stayed fixed on his wrist, clouding, growing distant. "My mother used to draw this image over and over after my father died. When I finally found the courage to ask her what it meant, she said that it stood for love's ability to rise above adversity and create positive change." He gave a melancholic chuckle. "I always assumed it represented my father, but now I'm not so sure."

I remained quiet, feeling the steady thump of my heart. My lips parted, hesitating only a moment before finally asking, "How did she die?"

Javier's body tensed, brows drawing forward as a frown consumed his lips. "No estoy seguro, mi vida. I'm not sure. She died when I was young, about six. At the time, General Harris was a Telvian Councilman. He got into an argument with her, and it got ugly. Shortly after that, Harris was demoted by my uncle to General of the REG, and then a week later, she was dead. I went to her room to wake her, but…" His voice dropped off, shaking his head lightly. "Ya estaba con mi padre. She was already with my father."

I pressed a hand over my mouth. "Javier, I'm…I'm so sorry."

He blinked, pupils dilating as he shifted his focus to me. "Don't be, mi vida. It was a long time ago."

"Do you…do you think he had something to do with it? Harris, I mean?"

Javier breathed in deeply. "Sí. Creo que le hizo algo. I think he did something to her."

I grimaced. How awful was that? To be forced under the command of the man you swore took your mother's life? And hell, no wonder why General Harris was such a prick. The guy was probably inches away from losing his status as a noble but ended up being humiliated and demoted instead. I blew out a breath, returning my gaze to the lotus. "I hope he gets what's coming to him," I muttered. "I seriously hope he rots."

Javier chuckled weakly. "I'd be lying to you if I didn't admit that visions of him in that fucking chair of his pleasures me almost as much as you do."

I frowned. "Not to judge your fantasies, Javier, but I'm not sure I like him and me sharing the same headspace."

He laughed then—a deep rumble that came out warm and true. "Dime, Javi, mi vida. Call me Javi. And don't worry," he said, reaching for me, pulling me against him once more. "I think I'd rather indulge in your pleasures now that I know how you taste." He nipped my lip, and I became a puddle of nothing once more.

22: Amor Vincit Omnia

Eventually he left me, and I had to face the day alone. Since he had the night shift, someone else came for me that afternoon long after he'd gone. Just like before, they took me to the chair. And just like before, Harris demanded my name. But I refused to cave, feeling renewed strength pumping through my veins—all from one night of desire and love.

I lasted only a few rounds before the black hedged at the corners of my mind, and I dove deep into the gloriousness of unconsciousness. Hours later, I awoke to find myself sprawled on my back, freezing. Time ticked, and eventually the shifts changed. The door to my cell unlocked, and I looked up from the corner to see Javier stepping in.

"Liddy?" he called, closing the door behind him.

I rose to my feet, shaky, hanging on to the wall for support. "Here…"

He closed the distance, pulling me into his chest. "Perdóname, mi vida. I'm so sorry I had to leave you."

I breathed deeply, filling my lungs with the scent of him. Holy stars, I loved how it felt to be held like this…held by *him*. "Then never do it again," I teased.

A low rumble of a chuckle emitted from him. He stroked my hair before taking my face into his hands. "I won't leave you again."

My heart melted—such a sweet sentiment. "I wish that were true."

He tucked a strand of my hair back. "I put a request in for overtime this week, and your usual guard owes me several favors."

My hands rested on his chest, feeling it rise with every breath. "Does that mean—"

"That I'll be serving as your jailer for the next week."

My chest tightened. "Won't Harris get suspicious?"

He rested his forehead against mine, thumbs stroking the lines of my cheek. "Don't worry about Harris. I'll take care of him. I just need you to stay alive, Lin."

Alive. I needed to stay alive, except…how much longer would I actually last? A lump formed in my throat as I shuttered, tipping my chin to my chest.

"Lin?" He dipped down, changing angles to get a better look at my eyes. "¿Qué te pasa, mi vida? What's wrong?"

My lashes fluttered as I tried to blink away my tears. "Amor vincit omnia," I uttered. "Love conquers all, right?" I sniffed. "Except love doesn't conquer death, does it?"

Javier's eyes widened, flaring bright like the sun glowing in the bluish-black of space. He cradled my face once more, tenderly forcing me to look at him. Every line was strong and rigid and firm. "Listen to me, Lin. You will not die. I won't let that happen, do you understand? I'm going to get you out of this. And when I do, we'll disappear. We'll fade from the memory of this world, and I will forever live in the temple of your love if you let me. But no matter what happens, have *faith*, mi vida. Tengas fe. You trusted me with your name, now trust me with your life. I *will* save you, Lin. I refuse to give myself another option."

Tears streamed down my cheeks. "Amor vincit omnia," I said through my tears.

"Amor vincit omnia," he whispered back. Then his lips crashed down upon mine, and I was lost once more to the ticking of time and the shadows of my captivity.

★★★

"Getting you out of your cell isn't the issue," he explained. "It's getting you out of the fucking camp that's the problem."

I sat cross-legged on the floor, watching him pace back and forth like a caged cougar. "Is there a way I could dress up as an officer? You said the schedules were chaotic, right? Maybe no one would notice me."

He shook his head. "Once you go topside, there are too many retinal scan checkpoints. You'll never make it past the first one." Back and forth, back and forth. "If there was a way to convince them you needed something…something that couldn't be provided to you down here. Like a scan or something."

I pursed my lips, thinking as I drew the bottled water Javier brought me to my lips. And then, *light bulb!* "Like a *medical* scan of some sorts? Or some sort of *medical* procedure?"

He stopped mid-step and looked at me. "*Yes?*" he drawled. "*¿Qué estás pensando?* What are you thinking?"

I hated doing this. It pulled Chase in without me having the chance to make sure he felt good about telling Javier he was helping me.

He'll understand, sis. Edith materialized from the corner, stepping forward.

Well where have you been? I accused, taking a sip from the bottle.

Tall, dark, and big stick over here seemed to have your emotional needs covered, she said, motioning towards Javier.

I almost choked on my water.

"Lin?"

I shifted my attention back to him. "I'm fine," I managed between gasps. "I may or may not have a friend who may or may not be able to help us out."

Javier folded his arms across his chest, squaring his shoulders. "You *may* have a *friend?*" Damn it, he looked hot standing like that. "What are you keeping from me, Lin?"

I blew out a breath. "I'm on Chase Beckham's roster for health assessments. He may have been helping me out by injecting me with saline instead of Everclear."

His eyes widened. "*Beckham's* your medical aid?"

"Maybe he can do something?" I said with a wince. "He's my friend. And just like you, he doesn't want to see me die in here. He'll help."

He cocked a brow. "Do I even want to know what your relationship with him *was* or *is* like?"

A lopsided smile curled my lips. "Are you *jealous?*"

He grinned. And it was a sexy, devilish grin that made my toes curl and my whole body quiver. He strode towards me. "I might be dissenting against my country, mi vida, but I'm still a de la Puente." He dropped right in front of me. "As it turns out, we don't share well."

I leaned back, resting my head against the stone wall. "You have nothing to worry about. I'm all yours. No sharing required."

"Good," he said, leaning forward. Arms caged me in on either side as Javier's lips brushed my own with every word. "Because I'm about to take what's mine."

Oh brother... Here we go again, Edith moaned. Then she disappeared back into the shadows.

***

Javier left my side early in the morning before shift changes. Even though I no longer felt his soothing presence, knowing he was just outside my door brought me comfort. We had agreed that roping Chase into our escape plan was our best bet. So when he arrived that morning for my routine check-up, I felt nervous as Javier followed him in and closed the door behind him.

"I'm here for your health assessment, Miss Huang," he said like usual.

"Chase," I began, not bothering to lower my voice this time. "Is there anything you can schedule me for that would give reason for me to go topside?"

He froze and the expression of utter shock would have made me laugh if this weren't such a serious conversation.

Way to ease him into it, sis, Edith scoffed in the corner. *And Mom always said I was the clunky one.*

I ignored her.

He just stared at me, eyes as big as saucers before he glanced over his shoulder at Javier, who was not helping to make this easy. He was standing there, feet shoulder width apart, arms crossed, head lowered, and a scowling face that would have sent a lesser person running home to their mommy.

"Well?" Javier said. "Answer her."

I sighed heavily, shoulders dropping. "You're not helping me right now."

Chase faced me again. "June?"

I shook my head, stepping forward and grabbing Chase by his shoulders. "He's going to help us. He understands the rotation schedule, and he thinks that if we can get me topside for a legitimate reason, then he might be able to sneak me out."

Chase looked like a damn ghost.

Can you blame him? Javier's the president's nephew. He grew up in the freaking Presidential Palace. You can't expect Chase to just incriminate himself like this, Edith admonished.

I blew out a breath. She was right. She was always freaking right. I looked at Javier. "Can you give us a minute?"

His gaze narrowed.

"*Please…*" I urged.

Several seconds passed until he finally nodded. "Knock when you're ready." With one more glance at Chase, Javier stepped outside.

Chase exploded. "Are you fucking *nuts*! What the hell are you doing?"

Here we go. "Chase, please, just listen. Javier is going to help me. He's going to help get me out, but we need—"

Chase shook out of my arms. "I can't believe you exposed me like that. I can't afford to be labeled a Dissenter, *June*."

"I know, and I'm sorry. But he's on our side—"

He glared. "He's a fucking *de la Puente*. He's one of *them*."

My hands curled into fists. "And what about Mara, huh? What about her? Last time I checked, she's a de la Puente too."

He faltered. "That's different. You know she's different—"

"Because she's *yours*?" I stepped forward, challenging him. "Javier's different too, okay? He's different, and right now he's the only thing keeping me from losing my damn mind in this place. Javier's offering me a chance to escape, and I'm taking it. But I need your help, Chase." I grabbed his hand and held it in both of my own against my chest. "Please…I need you."

He grimaced, worry carved on his brows. "What if he's using you? What if Harris has him cooking up this entire act just so you'll cave?" My heart stuttered. "What if it's all just so you'll give away everything he wants to know about you…everything you've been working so hard for?"

I stepped back, feeling shaken. Could it be? Could this whole romance between Javier and me be nothing more than an elaborate ploy cooked up by Harris?

I shook my head. No. I couldn't go down that road. I couldn't risk thinking that way. "He's…he's real," I insisted, but I would be lying if I said it was to convince Chase. "He's going to help me."

Chase remained silent for several minutes, and the tension throughout his body never eased. Finally, he spoke through his frown. "Look...I told you I would help you, and I will. But I can't do it and risk my future." He rubbed his chin for a moment and then blew out a breath. "I can figure something out. There are some new serums they're developing in the bio labs where Sally works. It might take me a few days, but I'll see what I can do."

"Thank you," I threw myself at him, wrapping my arms around his neck. I felt him hug me back, strong and firm.

"Don't thank me yet," he muttered as he let me go. "Harris is starting to suspect something with the serum. He's ordered me to increase your dose to two times the normal amount. I'm worried that if we don't get you out of here soon enough, he's going to do something rash."

I nodded. "Yeah, okay. What do you think we should do?"

His brows knitted together as he grimaced. "I don't know. But whatever it is, we're going to have to do it fast. I think our time's running out."

I've got a bad feeling about this, sis, Edith said from the edge of my consciousness. *A really bad feeling.*

I know, I replied. *I know.*

23: Dive

Later that afternoon, when my door opened, Javier's black gaze and a new officer greeted me. And when I saw the second, my heart screamed out a warning as every hair rose on the back of my neck.

"Well, well, well…what do we have here?" His deep voice reminded me of a bull. "A Huang?" Tim Harris laughed—a raucous rumble of mockery. "I've been waiting for over a week for rotation shifts. Looks like Christmas came early for me, huh?"

My instincts flared to life, and my fingers itched for my daggers, long gone. I'd forgotten that Tim had been assigned a career as a REG officer in the program. I should have at least suspected it that first day Javier showed up.

"I'd be lying if I said I was happy to see you, Harris. You look just as much as a prick as the last time I saw you."

He snickered. "Yeah, run that mouth of yours, Huang. Go ahead. I'm going to love watching you squirm—"

"Are we talking, Harris? Or are we working?" Javier cut in. "Last time I checked, we had a job to do." I could just hear the scowl in his voice. This was going to be the hard part…not giving away Javier's new allegiance to me and my welfare. No matter what happened, he couldn't intervene. He had to pretend like nothing existed between us.

Harris's face wrinkled as he spun the binders around his finger playfully. "So testy this morning, de la Puente. Didn't get enough sleep last night?"

Javier's gaze narrowed. "*Something* like that." He swiped the binders from Tim's hand just as Harris protested.

"Hey! I wanna do it—"

"Fuck off, Harris. I'm not in the mood."

Tim cursed under his breath, stepping toward the door where he waited. Javier faced me, giving Tim his back.

I whispered. "Careful…you can't give yourself away."

His anger was palpable as he worked his jaw. It was bothering him. This whole thing was bothering him. "Turn around, Huang," he snapped loud enough for Tim to hear, and then dropped his voice. "You have no idea how much this is gutting me right now. That I'm fucking handcuffing you and walking you to be tortured."

I turned around and offered a wrist. "I know. But you can't give yourself away," I repeated. "You can't help me if you're locked up too." The binding snapped around one wrist, then Javier reached for the other.

"Whatever happens, I'm here"—the restraint closed around my second wrist—"and when you wake up, I'll be here waiting for you."

I turned around, catching the pained expression worrying his brows. I wanted so badly to kiss him. To taste him. To collapse in his arms…but not now, not yet. Later, while my body recovered, I could feel safe in his embrace. It was the only light glimmering at the end of my torturous tunnel.

"Are we going, or what?" Harris snapped.

Javier scowled at Tim, but he kept his composure. Then, begrudgingly, he led me to Interrogation Room 4 to be tormented.

***

I was strapped to the chair, waiting for the incessant question Harris asked me over and over again. Just behind the general, Tim and Javier stood like sentinels. Tim picked his nails, sometimes his nose, but Javier was like a statue carved out of iron. His eyes found mine, and the anger in his face was devastatingly beautiful.

General Harris paced the platform, arms behind his back. "Now, my dear…I suspect today is going to be different. I have hope for you and your cooperation. Let's begin, shall we?" He stepped off the dais and walked behind the painted caution line on the floor. "Tell me the name of another rebel in Telvia."

Don't say anything, sis. Edith materialized from the shadows and stepped up onto the platform. She watched Harris like he was a snake preparing to strike.

I know. I remained quiet.

Harris glared. "No? How about the real name of May Huang? Tell me that."

Why is he asking something different? It's been days of the same damn question, and now it's something else.

Edith crouched beside me, taking my hand. *He's trying to confuse you. Just stay quiet.* I did as she said.

"Still no answer?" The general chuckled, a sardonic sound that made all the hairs on the back of my neck stand on end. "You are a stubborn thing, aren't you, Miss Huang?"

I glared at him.

His eyes landed on me as his lips curled into a frightening grin. "Or shall I say, Miss Liddy *Le*."

It was a sucker punch to the gut, causing my jaw to slacken. *But how…?*

Shit, Edith muttered beside me. *Somebody told him who you are.*

But nobody knows. Nobody knows but… I went cold. Completely drenched in ice from the tip of my toes to the top of my head. And then Chase's voice rang through my consciousness.

"What if he's using you? What if it's all just so you'll give away everything he wants to know about you…"

Oh shit, Edith said, standing up. *You don't think…?*

My eyes flew past Harris, finding Javier. And the look he gave me—that twist of angst and concern and guilt across his brow—it gutted me. *Oh my stars…was Chase right? Was Javier just using me?*

General Harris chuckled knowingly. "Ah yes, the look of discovering that those you've trusted have sold you out. It does hurt, doesn't it, Miss Le? Well, I hope you see that failing to answer questions here only leads to more pain and is ultimately just an act of martyrdom. I have ways of getting the information I need, my dear, whether or not you decide to cooperate. So you might as well just go along with it."

Tears flooded my vision as my throat closed up. *He betrayed me. He told Harris after I trusted him.*

Edith gripped my hand. *You don't know that, Lin. It could have been May—*

I shook my head. *If May had caved, then why would Harris bother questioning me? He would have everything he wanted. Javier fucking betrayed me!*

"Now, let's try this again, Miss Le. And remember, be honest." Harris rolled his shoulders back, standing proud. "What is your real name?"

I blinked, tears falling from my cheeks. "Fuck you, asshole."

Harris's face grew bitter. "Very well. Level 10, doctor." The whirring kicked up, and I saw as Edith backed away, a panicked look in her eye.

Find the black, sis. Find the black.

The electricity sizzled through me, and no matter how much I wanted to contain my scream, I just couldn't. It erupted from me with such ferocity, my vocal cords stung. I convulsed with the power coursing through my body, desperately searching for the black. And just before I found it, my eyes caught Javier's. Pure anguish was alight in the darkness of his eyes, and he looked as though he was ten seconds away from tearing the place apart.

Dive into the black, Lin! Dive! Edith screamed at me.

I did, and I faded into nothing.

24: Mi Vida

The cold woke me. My eyes fluttered open, finding myself curled on my side in my corner, resting on one blanket while being covered with the other.

He betrayed me.

It was the first thing that came back to my mind—the thought that Javier told General Harris my name. My vision was blurry, as it so often was whenever I woke from unconsciousness, and everything inside my body felt so cooked. I wasn't sure I could make anything respond but my eyes.

He used my heart against me.

I tried to move, my muscles groaning and aching with the effort. A whimper escaped me.

"Lin?" Male. Pained. Familiar. Gut-wrenching.

I searched the darkness, and the blurriness formed into a dark shape that moved toward me.

"Fuck, I thought you were never going to wake up." The strain in his voice—the utter breathtaking sound that was the fear and anguish in his accented voice—it stung my soul.

Slowly his shape cleared, and my eyes focused on Javier. Dark brows pinched. Frown curling the ends of his lips, contouring his beautiful face into a look of pain and concern. "Can you sit up, mi vida?" He reached for me, but I recoiled. "Lin?"

I forced my arms to obey, pushing hard to get them to push my body up. I whimpered from the effort—the pain—but I managed. "Don't touch me," I warned. "Don't you *ever* fucking touch me again." I sat myself up and flopped against the wall.

His head flinched back slightly, shoulders slackening. "Liddy?"

My eyes watered. "I can't believe I trusted you. That I thought you were different from the rest of them." My body threatened to fall over, but I caught myself with my arm, trying my best to hold firm. "You tricked me."

He shook his head. "What are you talking about?"

A bitter laugh escaped me. "You're such an ass, Javier. I should have known better than to trust you—"

"Lin!" he shouted as he grabbed my shoulders. "What are you talking about? I've done nothing to betray you—"

I tried to shrug him off, but my body was so weak from the electric shock, I could hardly move. "I told you not to touch me!"

He pulled back, hands lifting off and flying up in surrender. "Will you at least tell me what you think I did?"

I closed my eyes, feeling the tears pooling once more. Damn it, it hurt so much. Why did I have to fall for a pair of pretty eyes? *His* eyes? "You told him," I accused, glaring at him once again. "You told Harris my name."

Recognition crossed his face. "That's what this is about? You think I told Harris your name?"

I turned my face away from him, feeling a tear stream down my cheek.

"Liddy, I *never* told him. I've shared nothing about you."

I whipped around, setting a narrowed gaze on his handsome face. "Just go—"

"*Lin*," he raised his voice, gripping my shoulders once again. "You've got to believe me. I would never do anything to betray you."

I tried to shrug him off again, but this time, he refused to let me go.

"Mi vida, *please*, just listen to me," he begged. And *freaking hell*, the pain in his voice sounded so real. Like he was genuinely being gutted right here, right now, right before me.

I turned my face, closing my eyes as another stream of tears rolled down my cheeks. I couldn't bear to look at him. It hurt too much.

"I've never done anything to betray you. Not when Tim accused you of cutting him that day in the alley. Or when I discovered your blades and figured out who you were at the party. I've never reported *any* of it to *anyone*—"

"Stop it!" I refused to look. I couldn't. I *wouldn't*. The desperation in his voice was enough to have me gripping the end of my resolve.

"Liddy, *look* at me!" he yelled, shaking my shoulders. And I did look then. I looked right into his obsidian eyes and saw the torment writhing inside them. "You've got to believe me."

"Let *go* of me," I ordered, but my soul was cracking and breaking in two.

"I have *always* cared about you, Lin. From the first day I saw you, and every day thereafter, I have had eyes for only *you*. And I have called you only one thing since then—*one* thing."

My heart seized, and everything inside me stopped as though my very soul was holding its breath. "Mi vida," I whispered.

"My life," he said, the grip on my shoulders loosening. "Mi vida means *my life*."

Oh, holy stars…

"That's what you are to me, Lin. That's what you've *always* been to me…my *life*."

My soul shattered. It broke into a million finite pieces that I knew damn well I could never put together again. His hands dropped from my shoulders, and the blackness of his gaze glistened.

"It's why I let you go that night…why I never turned you in. You're my life, Lin. And I'll go to my grave first before I betray your trust."

I shivered, the remains of the adrenaline coursing through my veins. Javier took my hand in his and brought it to his lips, grazing my knuckles.

"Please, Lin, don't shut me out. Not like this. Not because you think I would hurt you this way." He kissed my hand—a sweet, gentle brush that would have brought me to my knees if I'd been standing. "Tengas fe en mí, mi vida. Have faith in me, and I promise I'll do everything in my power to earn your trust again"—another wisp of a kiss—"even if I did nothing to deserve losing it in the first place."

I wanted to resist him.

I wanted to hate him.

I wanted to revile him in every way I knew how.

But I couldn't.

I couldn't because I loved him. I was hopelessly and irrevocably in love with the man I'd been ordered to assassinate, and there was no going back.

"Please don't make me regret this..." I whispered, and even though I was speaking to him, I was truly speaking to my traitorous heart.

A tear left his eye as his face crumbled, and suddenly, I was in his arms, feeling the pounding of his heart against my chest. "The only thing I ever want you to regret is doubting me. But for my part, I will only ever honor you, Lin. Only ever love you. No matter what happens, my life is yours."

His lips found me then, and I allowed myself to be lost in the power of his love.

★★★

I was wrapped up in my blanket, alone in my cell. Javier was ordered to report in for some sort of mandatory training, but I knew he would be back before too long. The lack of nourishment pills was wearing on my strength. I didn't know if it was that, or the increase in voltage from the shock sessions, but it was taking increasingly longer for me to recover.

My mind was also troubled. There was a part of me that wanted to believe Javier wouldn't betray me, and I knew it was stupid of me to give in to him. But having him was a ray of hope that sustained me day after day. Losing that...? I didn't know if I could handle any more if I lost that brief glimmer.

But if Javier hadn't told Harris my name, who else was it? Who else knew?

It's gotta be May, Lin. Edith said, sitting next to me on the floor. *She's the only other person who makes sense, and Chase told you she wasn't doing well.*

But if she's talking, then why would Harris even bother with me? I argued.

Because he's a sick man who enjoys torturing you. I don't know. She shrugged. *Didn't you humiliate his son that day? Maybe this is payback under the guise of doing his job?*

Huh... That was a possibility. *But if that's true, there's no telling what else May has told him.*

Exactly, she agreed. *It's not enough to get you out of here, Lin. You've got to get May out, too, or she'll blow everyone's cover. It'll all go to hell.*

"You're right," I muttered. "You're always right."

What can I say? I'm awesome like that.

The door to my cell groaned, and light filtered in from the hallway.

"Good morning, Miss Le," a voice said. Female. Young. New. "I need you to stand, please."

"Who are you?"

The woman stepped further into the room, followed by Tim and Officer Cabrera. "She told you to stand," Tim growled. "So fucking *stand*."

Oh shit, Edith muttered as she stood. *Javier's not with them.*

Slowly, I stood, assessing the three individuals in front of me. "What's going on?"

Tim snickered, elbowing Cabrera. "We're doing things differently today, Le. And I think *I'm* going to like it."

This is bad, sis. Real bad.

I couldn't even respond to her. Before I could so much as breathe, both REG officers attacked me.

25: Payback's a Bitch

I tried to fight, but my body was so weak, it was pathetic. Tim came at me, but when I went to dodge him, Cabrera grabbed me, yanking my arms back.

Tim snickered, "Not so slick now, are ya, Le?" He circled me, slowly coming to stand in front. "Not such a badass anymore…" His storm gray eyes watched me.

POW!

A gut punch. I lurched forward, coughing and groaning from the strike. Freaking Harris hit like a hammer.

He shook out his shoulders, cracking his neck. "Did that feel good, Le? It felt good to me."

"Do it again, Harris," Cabrera goaded.

"*Oh yeah*, I'm gonna do it again," he bragged, then *WHAM*.

I yelped and then coughed, feeling my stomach clench and recoil. "You're such…an ass," I rasped out with ragged breaths.

"Officer," the girl squeaked out. "I'm supposed to—"

"Yeah, yeah," Harris waved her off. "Give me your arm," he snapped as he reached forward and grabbed my wrist. I resisted, but it was futile. Harris pulled out my arm, twisting it so the underside was exposed. "Do your job, medic."

The girl inched forward, lifting a syringe she had in her hand.

"What is that?" I struggled, but Cabrera grabbed me by my scalp and pulled back, making me clench my jaw.

"The general has ordered you to be given a triple dose of Everclear, miss." She tapped the syringe, making sure all the air bubbles left the needle.

I struggled, but Cabrera only twisted his hand in my hair further. "Where's Beckham?" I hissed.

"The peacock doesn't work today," Harris said, malice thick in his tone. "And Dad wants this done *now*." The girl positioned the needle at the crook of my arm.

"Please," I begged. "Don't do this!"

"I'm sorry," she said.

The needle pierced my skin, and unlike the saline, this serum burned. Fire coursed up my arm, through my shoulder. And when it hit my heart, it exploded in a thousand different directions, feeling like an inferno was raging in my blood. I shuddered in Cabrera's grasp.

The girl pulled out the needle and capped it. "I'm not sure what that'll do to her. We've never tested subjects with that much serum before."

Harris snickered. "Well, we're going to find out, now aren't we?" He looked at Cabrera. "Cuff her."

I felt the bindings snap on my wrists, and then Cabrera shoved me forward.

"No one's going to save you now, Le," Harris badgered. "Not even de la Puente's going to stop what's coming."

Edith! I screamed. *Help me!*

My sister materialized from the shadows, worry and fear etched on her brow. *I wish I could, Lin, but I can't. I'm just you. There's nothing I can do.*

And just like that, my sister vanished. Gone. And I knew I would never see her again.

★★★

I was strapped to the stupid chair once more, and my veins still felt like they simmered from the Everclear. Cabrera and Tim stood at the back wall, closer to the shadows, while General Harris stepped onto the platform.

"You've had an odd resistance to the Everclear, my dear. I thought it was time we upped the dose again." He turned to face the doctor. "We're moving to Stage 3, doctor."

The man in the lab coat gave a thumbs up and pressed several buttons. "We're ready, General."

"Excellent." General Harris stepped off the platform and walked behind the safety line. "We're going to do things a little differently, Miss Le. And depending on how cooperative you are, maybe a break from our contraption will be in order, yes? Doesn't that sound nice?"

My mind felt strange—fogged in a way—and my breaths were labored.

"Let's begin, shall we? What is your name?"

"Liddy Le." *Wait, what? Did I actually just say that?*

Harris smiled. "Excellent. Very good. Let's try something else." He placed his hands behind his back. "What is May's real name?"

"May Huang." *Oh my god! My mouth has a mind of its own.*

The general chuckled. "Very good, my dear. Very good indeed."

I quickly tried to cover my tracks. "How do you know? I could be lying."

The general shook his finger. "No, my dear. As it turns out, Miss Huang already confirmed her real name to me, just as she told me yours. And even if she hadn't"—he pointed to the doctor in the corner—"the doctor can tell from all the readings this brilliant machine takes from your body." He clasped his hands and rubbed them together. "So, let's keep going, shall we?"

It was May. May was the one who told Harris, not Javier. But I couldn't deal with that now. And I couldn't deal with the fact that May was a liability to the Dissenters. Because right now, *I* was a liability. If I kept blabbing, they were all in danger!

"How do the Dissenters get past the walls?"

"We have a series of underground tunnels. A network—" *STOP IT!* I screamed at myself. I bit my tongue, pressing my lips tightly together.

"A network of what? Please keep going, my dear. I'm absolutely riveted."

He tastes like mint. And when he kisses you, it's like the world has come to an end, and you are the only thing that matters to him.

"Speak, Miss Le. Tell me about the tunnels," he ordered.

I pressed down harder. *His hair feels like silk. His eyes are bottomless, black obsidian that seem to carry the weight of the world within them.*

Harris waved at the doctor, and the whirring sound fired up. Electricity sizzled through my body, harsh and intense as the day before, and I writhed uncontrollably against my bindings.

Twenty seconds…

Thirty…

Forty…

It stopped, and I went limp, panting like a dog.

"What are the tunnels?"

I squeezed my eyes shut, clamping down my mouth. *His skin is smooth against your touch, and when you brush your lips against his chest, against those three words written in black ink, he shudders beneath you.*

The whirring kicked up again just as I heard Harris shout, "Level 9!"

I shook and jolted and convulsed. Pain was a living, breathing dragon within me, burning my body, lighting me aflame, and I screamed.

Fifty…

Sixty…

Seventy…

It stopped.

Ragged breaths. My heart backfired, skipped a beat, and then pumped at an unnatural rhythm.

"The tunnels, Miss Le. What are the tunnels?"

His hands are strong when they lift you. And somehow, he fits so beautifully perfect in the V of your legs…so right. Like he was made just for you, and you for him.

The whirring fired up again, and the volts of electric shock vibrated through every nerve in my body. It was fire, pure *fire*, and embers and lava and magma—pumping, pushing, seething through my veins. I cried out, shrieking as my body lost all control, flailing in a sea of endless pain. *Where's the black? Why can't I find the black?*

"Sir! Any longer and we'll kill her like the last one—"

"Level 11!" Harris ordered.

The whirring intensified, and the pain magnified beyond belief, beyond any sense. But no matter how desperately I tried, I couldn't find the edge of my consciousness. I couldn't find the black! Another scream erupted from the depths of me, and the sheer power of it shredded my vocal cords.

"Sir, you're killing her!"

Eighty…

Ninety…

One hundred…

The whirring stopped, and I collapsed against my bindings once more. My heart kicked, jerked, jolted. Something wasn't right. It was struggling to keep going, struggling to find its rhythm. I closed my eyes, begging it to keep going, to keep beating.

"I didn't order you to stop!" the general screamed at the doctor.

"But, sir, her vitals are all over the place. I...I think you might have done permanent damage. Her heart can't take it—"

"Zap her again," he ordered. Shuffling. SMACK! "I said zap her *again*!"

"General Harris." A fresh voice. Loud. Male. Angry. Familiar. *Javier.*

I opened my eyes, and I almost broke out in tears at the sight of him. The door stood wide open, and filling the doorway was my dark knight. His eyes drifted over to me, and the quick flash of primal rage twisted the look on his face.

Harris whipped around to face him. "Ah, Officer de la Puente," he acknowledged. "You're right on time."

Javier narrowed his gaze but worked hard to control his temper. He stood up straight and lifted his chin. "I was told to report to you, sir. Prisoner JH4456 wasn't scheduled for interrogation today. May I ask what's going on?"

I struggled to look at Harris, but I caught the evil grin that curled on his lips. "That's above your rank, Officer." He stood up straight, placing his hands behind his back. "Step inside, Mr. de la Puente. I have a special task just for you."

That didn't sound good. That sounded downright diabolical.

Javier worked his jaw and risked a quick glance at me before stepping further into the room. I noticed Cabrera and Tim snickering in the corner. Javier trained his gaze straight ahead, never looking at the general. "What are my orders, sir?"

Harris motioned for the doctor to step away from the computer. "I thought that a celebrity, such as yourself, deserved the opportunity to test out our beloved president's greatest invention." He placed a hand on Javier's back while lifting the other, motioning to the computer.

Javier clenched his jaw. "I'm not qualified."

"Nonsense. No qualifications necessary."

Javi's chest rose with a steady breath. "Miss Le looks as though she is a poor test subject, sir. Unfit for any further research. Perhaps another day—"

"Enough!" Harris snapped. "Consider this an order, Officer de la Puente."

Javier scowled. "But, sir—"

"Follow directions, de la Puente. You're starting to remind me of your mother."

Javier whipped his head around, facing Harris with a glare. "Care to clarify, General? I'm afraid I don't understand your meaning."

He sneered. "Don't act stupid with me. Your uncle might have been blind to her associations, but I knew damn well the company she kept." He pointed to the computer. "Do your job, Officer." His eyes glinted with evil delight. "Or are you refusing to do your duty?"

Oh blessed stars…please tell me this wasn't happening. Every line of his body was like perfectly sculpted ice. I could see his jaw working, see the internal battle within him. If he refused, what would happen to him? Would Harris figure out that Javier was dissenting?

Damn it! I hated this! He had to do it. He had to follow orders, or it would all be lost!

With the little energy I had, I muttered out a few words—anything to get his attention and hopefully keep Harris off the scent. "What's…the matter…Javier? Too much…of a…pretty boy?"

Javier faced me, eyes burning bright. Lips pressed into a thin line.

General Harris narrowed his gaze at me. "You are a masochistic thing, aren't you, Miss Le?"

But I wasn't listening to him. All I cared about was Javier right in front of me. The tight lines across his face. The glisten of perspiration on his brow.

I muscled my vocal cords to obey. To say those last two words that I knew he needed to hear. "Do it."

His brows drew forward into a deep V, and with a scowl painted on his face, he stepped over to the computer and looked straight into my eyes. "Perdóname."

Javier pushed the button, and the machine whirred to life.

26: Perdóname

To say that my body lit up like a damn Christmas tree would have been putting it lightly. I thrashed so hard against the leather straps, I never felt how they bit into the flesh of my wrists. My bones clacked against the metal collar, but I couldn't even register the pain of it while endless volts of electricity shot through my body, causing me to scream out louder than I ever had before.

Ten seconds...

Twenty-five...

Thirty...

"*Enough*, General," Javier yelled.

"*I'll* say when it's enough!" He yelled back.

My scream pierced my own ears, and the very tears in my eyes felt like they were burning my pupils, sizzling my corneas.

"General!" Javier yelled again.

Fifty-five...

Seventy-five...

Eighty...

"*Fuck.*" I heard that beautiful voice cry as my chest heaved.

"Increase to Level 12, de la Puente!"

Ninety...

Ninety-five...

"Fuck *no!*"

"Don't you dare defy me. That's an *order*! *Do* it."

Oh god, I didn't know if I could take any more. But he *had* to. There was no way out of this!

"*Shit*," he shouted, piercing his hand through his hair.

"*Now!*" Harris's voice cracked like thunder, but I hardly heard him over my cries.

The machine gave a high pitched shrill, louder than before, and my entire body arched unnaturally in the chair, the collar digging into my neck.

"You're fucking killing her!"

Two minutes…

"Enough!" Harris finally said.

The machine whirred down, and volts finally stopped coursing through me. My body jerked irregularly in the chair. My heart thumped weakly, abnormally.

Thump…thump…thump.

My breaths were ragged, pained, shallow, and useless.

The general placed his hands behind his back as he stepped onto the dais. "I think you need to reconsider your defiant nature, Miss Le. I doubt that next time you'll be so lucky." He turned, stepped off the platform, and walked toward the door. "Officer Harris, Cabrera, follow me." He walked to the door, his stooges in tow. "Oh, and Officer de la Puente…lovely work today. I expect you to do it again tomorrow."

Javier's face paled.

He laughed. The freaking general laughed and walked out the door.

The doctor squeaked from the side, entering my field of vision. "What about the girl, Officer? She's…she's…"

"She's *what?*" Javier growled. The doctor stepped behind the computer, and both stared at the screen. They muttered back and forth, and at one point, I swore I heard Javier curse before he finally nodded. The doctor left the interrogation room, and then Javier walked toward me, stepping onto the platform. He crouched down before me. "Hey," he whispered.

I sniffed. "I can't lift my head," I whimpered. It was tipped at an angle, the collar digging into my neck. "Everything hurts so bad, Javi. And my heart…it feels like it's broken."

His eyes glistened, reflecting the light of the contraption. "I know, Lin." He took my hand and kissed it. "I'm so sorry. I'm so sorry for what I've done. I hope you can forgive me, mi vida."

"It's okay," I sniffed. "You had to."

He shook his head, and the agonizing look on his face made me feel like my heart was breaking all over. "Let's get you out of this, okay?" he whispered.

"Okay," I murmured, a tear rolling down my cheek.

He brushed it away softly and then started undoing my restraints. The last thing he unlatched was my metal collar, and when he did, I collapsed into him, completely limp.

"I'm scared," I whispered. "My heart feels weird—irregular—and my chest hurts."

Javier leaned, scooping up my legs with one arm, while diving the other behind my back, then lifted. He tucked me into him, my head limp on his shoulder. "You're going to be okay, Lin. I'll make sure of it. Just keep fighting for me, okay? Can you do that?" He moved quickly, rushing me out of the room and down the hall.

"I don't know." It was the truth. The Liddy from yesterday would have said *yes*. But she didn't know what today would bring. She didn't know just how far the torture and torment would go. Just how much it would hurt and break her. She didn't know that she *could* be broken.

"Don't talk like that, Lin. You're a fighter. You always have been. I just need you to fight a little longer." Down another hallway, then a sharp left. "You can do that for me, right? You can fight."

Thump. Ka-thump.

My heart backfired again...weaker this time. And each beat thereafter felt like it was losing strength.

Thump. Thump.

"I-I think my heart is slowing down. It's hardly beating." Stairs. He was carrying me up a flight of stairs.

"We're almost to the medical unit, Lin. Keep fighting. Don't give up." He kicked open a door and jogged down another hallway.

Thump. Thump.

The world started spinning, and my chest ached. "Javier..."

"Fight, mi vida. *Fight!*" he growled, pushing through another door.

Thump...Thump...Thump...

"I'm sorry," I whispered, and then my eyes rolled back as my head flopped off his shoulder.

"*Lin!*"

And then I was gone.

27: Cheeseburgers = Freedom

"You'll never get her out of here like this. She's too weak. The Everclear isn't reacting well in her system, and I don't think her heart can take another round of interrogation." Male. Deep. Familiar. Frustrated. *Chase.*

"*Fuck.*" One syllable, and then a clattering of objects hitting the floor. "You better have answers for me, Beckham. Because I guarantee Harris is going to put her in that chair again tomorrow." Male. Familiar. Safe. Accented. *Javier.*

"I've done some research... There's a serum being worked on in the bio lab derived from deadly nightshade. If I dose it right, it'll put her in a catatonic state, making it look like she's dead."

Making me look like what? Were they talking about me? I tried to move, but my body refused to respond. I couldn't even open my eyes.

"Then she'll be removed from the cell and taken topside," Javier muttered.

"Exactly." A pause. "But I can't give it to her yet. Not like this. She needs to regain some of her strength—"

"*Pero no tenemos tiempo*...we don't have time," Javier growled. "Don't you get it?"

Another pause. A blown-out breath. "Listen, Harris needs her alive and strong enough to be questioned, right? I'm going to recommend several days of respite for her to recover. In the meantime, you've got to get your hands on that serum."

"How?"

"Sally was assigned to the bio labs at Initiation. She can get it for you," Chase whispered.

Quiet. One second… Two seconds… "Wouldn't it make more sense for you to contact her?"

A low growl. "I can't afford to be accused of dissenting, de la Puente. Liddy knows that. Once you're both out of here, you're gone. But I have to live with whatever the consequences are, and then who's going to help me if I'm suspected of helping you guys escape?"

Silence once again, then finally, "Te entiendo…I understand. I'd appreciate whatever help you can give us."

Shuffling. I tried to open my eyes again, but I couldn't. Blackness swirled at the edge of my consciousness.

Chase began whispering once more. "Over the next few days, I'm going to give her something extra—"

"*Extra*? What do you mean, *extra*?"

"Look, I don't like you, de la Puente," Chase grated out. I could hear his annoyance, practically see the scowl on his face in my mind's eyes. "And I sure as hell don't trust you. I'm doing this for *her*, not you. So shut up, and *don't* push me." Tension. Quiet for several irregular heartbeats.

"Fine."

"All you need to know is that after I dose her, she's going to be in and out of consciousness, so don't freak out. In five days, she's going to be ready to fight her way out of here, and I'm going to have to report that she's ready for interrogation in order to avoid suspicion. Understand?"

"Got it."

"You better be ready with the nightshade by then. The morning she's scheduled for interrogation, I'll dose her with nightshade instead of Everclear. Once she's out, I'll pronounce her dead."

Quiet.

Several breaths.

"Are you sure this will work?"

"If it doesn't, she's going to end up in a body bag just like May." Silence. "Five days, de la Puente. You've got to be ready to get her out in five days."

"Amor vincit omnia," he uttered so low, I almost thought I imagined it.

"What?"

"I said, I'll be ready."

I tried to hang on to consciousness, but for once I didn't have to search for the black. It swirled over the edges of my mind and consumed me whole.

***

I awoke lying on my side, shivering. My fingers twitched first, then my toes, and then my lungs inflated with a sudden painful inhalation of air as my eyes opened wide.

"Lin," Javier said, filling my vision as he leaned in to look at me. "Gracias a dios, you're awake."

I panted, my heart thumping oddly in its cage, causing me to wince. "Javier?" I tried to sit up, gripping my chest as I did.

He reached out to help me, and like so many times before, I ended up slumped against the wall. My breaths were ragged this time, however. That was new.

"Why does my heart feel like a beat-up truck that keeps backfiring?"

He stroked my hair, then caressed my cheek. "Cardiac arrhythmia, mi vida. It's a side effect of the electroshock. It should have gone away by now, but Chase thinks Harris overdosed you with Everclear and it's prolonged the side effects."

"Well, that sounds fan-flipping-tastic," I groused as I closed my eyes and tried to focus on slow, steady breaths. "How long have I been out?"

"Four days."

My eyes shot open. "*What?*"

"Listen, we don't have much time, mi vida. Tomorrow, Chase is coming to assess you and clear you for interrogation. He's going to dose you with—"

"Nightshade...I know the plan."

"What? How?" Javier looked at me like I was a cheeseburger dancing a jig.

"I overheard you guys talking. I couldn't move anything, but I could still hear you." I shifted on the floor, stretching my legs out before me. Huh? Nothing hurt. I rolled my shoulders and stretched my arms. "Wow," I mumbled. "I feel good. If it weren't for the pain in my chest, I'd feel like running a marathon."

Relief washed over his face with a sigh. "Do you feel strong enough to fight?" He took my hands in his, lifting my right and brushing his lips against my knuckles.

I thought about that for a moment, mentally checking my body. "Yeah, I think so. Did you get the nightshade?"

He nodded. "Sí. Tu amiga me ayudó."

"English," I reminded him.

He chuckled, then brushed the back of his fingers across my jaw. "I got it. Sally helped me out and had it delivered to me this morning."

I leaned into his hand. "What did you tell her?"

"That I needed it for something at the camp."

"That easy, huh? Is that typical?"

He shrugged. "Too easy, right? There's a protocol to get serums, and the medical assistants are the ones that make the request. That's why I think Chase should have done it—"

I shook my head. "He can't be involved in this anymore than he already is, Javi."

He scrutinized me for a moment. "He's one of you, isn't he? He's a Dissenter."

I looked him right in the eye, my voice stern. "Don't ask me questions like that. Whether he is or isn't doesn't matter. Would you want either of your cousins put in Chase's position? Would you ask *them* to risk themselves for you?"

All suspicion fell from his face as he shook his head. "No, I wouldn't."

"It's the same thing. Chase is committing treason against Telvia for helping me. The day he gave me saline instead of Everclear was the day he dissented. Who he was before is irrelevant."

He worked his jaw for a moment. Then something shifted within him. Heaviness fell upon him as he moved to sit beside me. "Lin, I've been thinking about what happens after…" his voice trailed off as I rested my head on his shoulder, and then felt the pressure of his head resting on my crown. "I'm…" he faltered—only a moment. "I'm not ready to dissent…not like that."

My heart thumped irregularly, causing my chest to tighten. Somehow, even though Javier had cast his loyalties for his country aside, I knew he wouldn't become a Dissenter. One thing was saving me. Another was agreeing to join in a full out war against his uncle. "Because of your uncle, right? Your cousins?" They were his family after all. The only family he had left.

"My uncle might be wrong, mi vida, but deep down, he's not a bad man. There's good in him still, he's just lost."

I snorted. "That's saying it lightly."

He squeezed my hand. "I know he's done terrible things, but it's not just him, Lin. I can't fight a battle that might cause harm to Jacob and Mara." He shifted under me. "Mara's life is already hell, and Jacob's a REG officer now too. I can't risk hurting him." He moved, pulling away and turning to face me. And the look in his eyes—the look of pure sacrificial love—it took my breath away. "But you can go home, Lin. You can go home and be with your family. I'll be fine on my own."

My chest tightened, but not from the arrhythmia that caused my heart to stutter. But because Javier was sacrificing himself for me. *Damn him and his willingness to put me first.* Who the hell would I be if I did that to him? To allow him to lose everything for me, only to make him walk this world alone?

I shook my head. "No. No, I'm not doing that to you—"

"Lin," he said, shoving his hands through his hair. "Be reasonable—"

"I *am* being reasonable." I shifted onto my knees, sitting on my legs as I gripped his hands in mine. "You're giving everything up for me. Why?"

"Don't…" he muttered, pulling away.

I reached forward and cradled his face in my hands, forcing him to look at me. "Because you love me, right? You *love* me. And love conquers all," I said, placing a hand over his heart."

"And apparently good judgment," he snarked.

I smiled. "And apparently good judgment," I agreed.

He took my hand from his heart and brought it to his lips once again. "We'll have to disappear. You know that, right?"

The image of my sister came to mind, and the ache in my chest intensified. "I know." I let the thought rest heavy on me for a moment. "Maybe, once this is all over, I'll see them again. There's an entire world out there, Javi. So big and vast"—I laughed softly—"you're not going to know what to do with yourself."

He chuckled, settling back against the wall once more. "It's hard to imagine actually…that there's anything beyond the desert."

I cuddled up next to him. "Just wait until you taste a cheeseburger—"

"A what?"

"A cheeseburger. It's food, and it's orgasmic."

He tipped his head back and laughed. "*Orgasmic* food? Are you telling me I'm competing against this cheeseburger for your affection? Please tell me there's no comparison…"

"Uh, I'm going to decline answering that question—"

"What!" He spun on me, laughter rumbling from him as he struck out with his fingers, tickling my sides. "Take it back, mi vida, or suffer the consequences."

I fell onto my back in a fit of giggles, as Javier came over me, never ceasing. "All right! All right! I take it back! You're the Orgasmic King! Cheeseburgers hold no quarter over you."

Finally he stopped, and my poor heart backfired with an irregular beat, causing my chest to twinge. Javier brought his lips to mine, pressing them gently against me. He flashed me a cocky grin as he whispered, "Orgasmic King, you say? I like this new title. Me gusta mucho," he purred, taking my bottom lip between his teeth.

"Yeah? Well *me gusta mucho,* too, your majesty. Don't let it go to your head."

His knee parted my legs, and suddenly he was resting in between my thighs while a hand slowly traveled up my hip. "Demasiado tarde por eso, mi vida." His voice sounded like silk and sinful melted chocolate. "Too late for that," he translated as that hand journeyed under the hem of my shirt.

It took all of one irregular heartbeat before I was lost in the sensuousness of my chosen future…a lifetime of Javier de la Puente. And as I allowed him to dive deep into the depths of me, my heart stuttered and pounded its unnatural dance. All we had to do was survive tomorrow.

We could do that.

We could make it.

We had to.

28: This Is It

Javier spent much of the rest of the day gone from my cell. Before he left, he brought me extra nourishment pills and instructed me to get plenty of sleep. When I asked him where he was going, all he said was "Plan B…just in case." That evening, after the whole camp was quiet for the night, he slipped back in, and we reviewed the plan for what felt like the billionth time.

"No te asustes, mi vida. Don't be scared."

"I'm not afraid of the dark, Javi. I'll be fine," I replied tartly. I didn't want to be snappy, but my MO was always to get a little snippy before a mission—my way of managing the adrenaline and angst that could save your ass when you needed it, or ruin you if not kept in check. Keeping it in check for me was allowing myself to be a little bitchy.

Not the best way, I know. But my way, nonetheless.

Javier cocked a brow at me but didn't push it. *Smart man.* "Beckham or I will make sure there's a hole in the bag so you can breathe. But remember, whatever you do—"

I waved my hand in a circle flippantly. "Don't get out of the bag before you arrive. Yeah, yeah. I got that." He narrowed his eyes. I ignored him. "How long before you arrive?"

"Hopefully within the hour. They'll call me in for a brief interview about it and then assign me a new post. That's when I'll head to the morgue to get you."

I nodded.

He pointed to a crudely drawn map he'd brought, hidden in the folds of his uniform. We were both sitting side by side, eyeing the schematic. "There are two morgues in the facility. One's below, and the other is topside. We only use the one below if the one on top is full."

I cocked a brow.

He tipped his head, eyes trained on the map, as he answered my silent question. "It's colder the deeper underground you go. If we're backed up on incinerating the bodies up top, the cold temperatures below act as a natural refrigerator of sorts. Keeps the bodies—"

"From rotting," I cut in, wrinkling my nose. "How often do you guys lose so many inmates that you need a freaking back-up morgue?"

He grimaced. "Enough."

Yuck, and also, I fucking *hate* Telvians.

Javier pressed on. "The morgue is at the back of the facility, but if I timed this right, we'll be coming up onto shift rotation, so that'll help." He shoved his hands into his hair, blowing out a breath. "The most direct route is going to take us through several retinal scans, and I can't bypass those. We're going to have to snake through the facility to avoid them."

I rocked back on my bottom, straightening my back to ease the tension clawing its way up my spine. "Any chance this is easy?"

Javier looked at me. "Ni un poquito, mi vida. Not even a little bit."

Well, that's not comforting. "You could have lied to me, you know? Save me the grief."

A grin curled the corners of his tasty lips. "Something tells me you're not the kind to be coddled."

I smirked. "And that is one of several reasons why I love you."

"Please tell me the other reason is because I outperformed a fucking cheeseburger earlier?"

I patted his cheek with a wicked smile. "Something tells me you're not the kind to be coddled."

He sighed heavily, hanging his head with a chuckle. "Por dios, este cheeseburger debe ser asombroso."

"Meaning?"

He snickered. "Basically, cheeseburgers must be awesome."

I laughed. It was funny to think that if someone had told me a month ago, I would find myself head over heels for the president's nephew, I would have punched them in the face. Life certainly had a way of taking you places you never would have thought possible.

After our laughter settled for a moment, I cleared my throat and got back to the business at hand. "What happens once we're out? I don't even know where this stupid camp is."

"We're outside Telvia's walls. The problem is everything is desert for miles as far as the eye can see. Beckham told me to head east, to meet him where the road winds and points north. He said you would know what that means."

I smiled. I *did* know. *Freaking Chase...you're a damn saint.* "When we're out, I'll lead the way then."

"Want to enlighten me, mi vida?"

"Nope," I said with a smile as I folded his map and tucked it in his shirt.

He shook his head, grumbling. "Esta mujer me va a matar..."

"Hey," I whined, curling my fingers around the collar of his shirt. "What's that supposed to mean?"

He smirked, eyes drifting to my lips. "It means you're going to kill me."

"Nope. Been there, opted out," I said lightly, as though me choosing *not* to kill him that night was no different from choosing not to wear pink. "And besides, I still have hopes for you to out-perform that cheeseburger one day." Then I pulled him down to my mouth, drawing his bottom lip between my teeth.

"Dicen que, al practicar, uno mejora su jugo..."

I tipped my head, lining up our lips better, savoring the minty taste of him. "Meaning?"

His hands wrapped around my waist and pulled me into him. "Rough translation...practice makes perfect."

"I admire your dedication."

***

The following morning, my heart was still struggling to find its natural rhythm. Javier said Chase had hoped it would stabilize with the *extra* serum he gave me, but I was still struggling. When my cell door opened, Chase came in, followed by Javier and freaking Harris.

I glared at him.

"Well good morning, Liddy *Le*. Ready to be a good girl for my dad today?" Tim always had a thick, husky voice, which suited his body well since the man was a human tank. But something about it sounded a pinch too high.

"What's wrong, Tim? Struggling to find your courage since your buddy isn't here to back you up?" I stayed back in my cell, wanting Chase to have to come toward me. I wasn't even a little afraid of Tim. But I wanted to talk to Chase, and that would be better accomplished with him coming my way.

Tim cleared his throat, but it still sounded a smidge high for my liking. "I don't need back-up to take you out, Le," he growled.

"Really?" I let out a mocking bark of a laugh. "That's truly funny, because the only time you've faced me by yourself, you ate shit. Every other time, you needed goons to hold me down for you."

His face grew beet red as his fingers curled into massive fists at his side. "I'm going to destroy you, Le. And I'm going to enjoy every fucking second of it."

Chase looked between us, but quickly walked to me, carrying his bag.

"Yeah, well make sure your balls drop first, you jerk. Have the guts to face me without Cabrera holding me back—"

"What?" Javier whirled on Tim, stepping into him and shoving him back. "What the fuck is she talking about, huh? What the fuck did you and Cabrera do?"

Tim growled. "Get your hands off me, de la Puente. I don't answer to you!"

Chase was suddenly in my field of vision as the other two started arguing. He whisper-yelled at me, "Do you really need to pick a fight with him right now?"

"Yes," I groused.

He rolled his eyes, going through the motions of his health assessment. I tried to look over his shoulder, catching Tim shove Javier back. "*Focus*," he snapped at me as he kneaded my neck. I dragged my eyes to him. "Did he tell you where to meet me?"

I nodded, feeling as he performed the crappiest, least thorough exam ever. He wasn't even bothering with his stupid stethoscope.

"If for some reason I can't meet you when you get there, check under the Joshua Tree. There will be a bag—some money and clothes for you."

I nodded, watching him pull out the syringe from his bag. "Thank you."

He smiled weakly. "Don't mention it. Where will you go?"

I shook my head. "I'm not sure. Someplace where he won't be recognized. He'll be a target if anyone realizes he's Raúl's nephew." I extended my arm, giving him easy access to the sensitive skin where I knew his needle needed to find a vein.

Chase searched for his mark. "I'm going to miss you, Lin. But I'd rather you alive and never see you again than here suffering or dead."

I smiled, feeling my heart thump oddly. "I'm going to miss you, too. Thank you for everything you've done for me."

He nodded with a weak smile. Finding the vein, he lined up the needle.

"Hey, I hope you capture her heart, Chase. I hope Mara falls in love with you like I—" I stopped, looking over his shoulder at a very pissed off looking Javier. They had finally stopped arguing, but the scowl on Javi's face had him looking like he was about to crack a molar and set the world on fire.

"Thanks, Lin." The needle pierced my skin, and I winced. "I'll start courting her soon. She won't be eligible for matching until she Initiates, but I want to be someone she chooses, not someone she's forced to be with."

I smiled. "She's going to be madly in love with you. Just wait and see." The nightshade felt cool, like ice sliding up my arm. Such a sharp contrast to the burn of the Everclear. As it neared my heart, I knew I was running out of time.

"Chase," his green eyes found mine. "If you ever see my sister, please tell her I'm sorry."

The cold hit my heart, and with the next *ka-thump*, it spread like glacier ice throughout my body. Chase's eyes flickered, filling with grief. "You'll tell her yourself one day. Bye, Lin."

"Goodbye, Cha—" I blacked out.

★★★

My eyes opened, but I saw nothing but darkness. Fear fluttered through my heart.

Stay calm. Keep it together. You're in the body bag, just like we planned.

I didn't dare move a muscle. It was stuffy and oddly humid, but I remained still as I listened hard for any sounds.

Silence.

I scanned my little cocoon. A glimmer of light shone just above my crown. *Yes, the gap in the zipper they promised.* The gap did little to light my world, though, and after several moments of sitting in the dark, the bag felt like it was closing in on me, making me restless.

But I waited.

Minutes passed.

Time ticked, but I stayed still…waiting.

And then I just couldn't wait anymore. It was hot and sweaty, and the air felt stale and suffocating despite my stupid little hole in the zipper. I just couldn't do it anymore.

Oh hells to the no.

I closed my eyes and listened for several more seconds. When I didn't hear a single sound, I drew my hand up my chest and prodded the hole, poking my finger through. Working the zipper, it slowly inched open, and cold air caressed my cheeks. I breathed in, relishing the fresh oxygen. With one more push, the zipper pulled back far enough that I could stick both my hands through, and then tug. The zipper groaned as it slid back and the sides opened, letting me free.

Thank you stars and cheeseburgers everywhere.

Slowly, I sat up and took in my surroundings. I was sitting on a metal gurney of sorts. The head of my gurney was lined up with the blackened mouth of an incinerator, which currently stood cold and quiet. I shivered. I was in a crematorium. I pulled my legs out of the bag and swung them off the side of the gurney. The room was empty of any other body bags that I could see, and everything had a shade of gray, as though soot was shading the white walls.

"Javier?" I whispered, looking around. The room was empty—*quiet*. There was no furniture, no tables and chairs, nothing where anyone could hide.

Thump, thump…thump…thump, tha-thump.

My chest twinged with the irregular beat, and my hand flew to my heart, gripping the fabric of my shirt. Where was he? He was supposed to meet here, right?

I blinked, stepping off the gurney as my mind ran through the details of the plan. *Shit, did I screw this up? Did I remember something wrong?*

Thump…thump…thump, thump.

"Javier?" I whispered fruitlessly, as though just saying his name would make him materialize.

Damn it. Where the hell was he?

As though the universe was answering my question, the door to the room creaked and opened. I inhaled sharply, holding my breath. *Please be him…please be him,* I chanted.

The door swung wide, and my eyes fell on storm-gray ones. "Well, look at that," Tim Harris said. "Looks like the bitch was on to something."

My heart kick-started in my chest, pain strangling my breath. I looked around, but there was no way out, no escape. No windows, no other doors but the one Tim stood in. And there was absolutely nothing I could use as a weapon. The room was devoid of everything but the stupid gurney.

The smile that curled on his face was so smug, I had the biggest desire to smack it right off. Tim lifted his hand and aimed his gun at me. "Time to go, Le. Daddy's waiting for you."

Damn it, what went wrong? I hesitated, looking around one more time to see if there was anything I could do.

"Don't even think about it. Make one false move, and I'll put a bullet through your head. And besides," he snickered, "you'll miss the big surprise."

Slowly, I lifted my hands in surrender. As much as I hated to admit it, Tim-fucking-Harris had me beat. "What are you talking about?"

He shrugged, a sinister, gleeful look in his eyes. "Like I said, it's a surprise," he said jovially. "Now move it."

I swallowed. This was bad…really freaking bad.

Tim cocked back the hammer of his gun. "I said *let's go*," he barked at me.

"All right, Tim," I acceded. "Let's see your dad."

I took slow steps toward him, but he never made the mistake of getting too close to me, much to my chagrin. We left the crematorium. I walked the tunnels, taking the all-too-familiar path to the room that had been my personal hell.

God, I hoped he was just detained…stuck being interviewed for my presumed death. I couldn't imagine what else would keep Javier from meeting me on purpose, and I refused to let my mind wander anywhere dark. I couldn't afford dark thoughts right now. I had to stay focused. I had to figure out a way out of this mess.

I approached the formidable steel door to Interrogation Room 4. Gritting my teeth, my mind whirled with the same questions over and over again. How the hell did this happen? Where in the freaking hell did we go wrong? Where was Javier?

The barrel of Tim's gun dug into the back of my head. "Open the door," Tim ordered.

I bared my teeth. "*You* open it, you asshole."

Tim smacked the side of my head with the butt of his gun. I grunted as searing pain whipped through my consciousness. "Now open the fucking door," he ordered again.

Ka-thump…thump, thump.

My chest twinged. Reluctantly, I did as I was told. My hand touched the cool steel handle and turned it. The door swung open, and as I stepped inside, my heart nearly gave out. Because there, sitting in that fucking torture chair, was Javier.

29: Choices

General Harris stood before me, looking too proud of himself as freaking Tim continued to hold the barrel of his Glock against my temple. It was just the four of us. No doctor this time. Just Tim, his father, Javier, and me. And Javi looked like crap. A split lip and bruising across his cheek told me he didn't go down without a fight, but he was alive—for now—and that was the only part that mattered to me.

His obsidian eyes caught mine. "Perdóname, mi vida."

I offered him a weak smile.

"Aw yes, such sweet sentiment. It would seem the two of you were planning to leave without saying goodbye."

I tore my gaze away from Javier, dragging it back to the general.

"How impolite, my dear, considering we've all spent so much quality time together," he chastised.

What the hell happened? How did this all fall apart? I lifted my chin, standing tall. "Will you at least tell me how you figured it out?"

The general's lips curled into a wicked smile. "Why, Miss Le, I'm so glad you asked." He placed his hands behind his back as he walked toward me. "Miss Sally Miller, of course."

The color drained from my face as Tim snickered at my side. "No…" I whispered.

Harris, Sr. gave me a mocking frown. "I'm afraid so, my dear. It turns out Miss Miller is an astounding young woman who refuses to risk her newly obtained status as a District 2 citizen."

My fists curled at my sides. "Sally would never—"

"Oh, but she would, Miss Le," Harris said, cutting me off. "She would, and she did." He lifted his hands out to the side, palms out, with a crooked smile. "And honestly, who could blame her? The poor thing suffered in District 3 long enough and worked very hard to earn her way into 2. Really, if you think about it, *you're* the horrid friend for putting her in the position to begin with. For making her risk her own life to aid you two."

I grimaced, shoulders sagging. *Oh Sally…*

She didn't know, my intuition offered. *She didn't know she would be betraying you.*

Harris paced in front of me, hands behind his back once more. "Miss Miller thought it odd that our camp would request a serum still under study. So she did the honorable thing…she sent a query to the REG. And seeing as how *I'm* the general of the Rebel Enforcement Group, imagine my surprise when I was informed of such a request from this particular camp." He chuckled sardonically.

My brain was working overtime, racing to put the pieces together. *If Sally told him about the nightshade request, then he knew Javier was the one that asked for it.*

"*His* involvement," the general said as he pointed to Javi, "was not a surprise to me, my dear. And seeing how he was always so hesitant to do his work when it came to you, I put the pieces together quite easily." He clasped his hands together, rubbing them lightly. "After all, it wouldn't be the first time Javier had come to your defense, hmm? The incident in the alley was only the first time I suspected you and then subsequently *him*."

Damn it! This couldn't be happening. It couldn't end like this…

"My only hesitation with him was his surname," the general explained. "Officer de la Puente is quite beloved by his uncle, it would seem. And voicing my suspicions without proof…" he faltered, rubbing his chin as his eyes clouded over. "Well, let's just say that the president doesn't take kindly to such accusations."

My eyes widened momentarily as another light bulb went off. This wasn't the first time Harris had accused Javier of dissention. "This isn't about me, is it?" I said.

Harris's eyes flickered, coming back into the present, and narrowed on me.

"It's about him," I added, ticking my chin toward Javier. "You've been after *him* this whole time." My mind raced, snapping pieces together faster than I could get them out. "You've been using me to get him to break, haven't you? That's why you insisted on questioning me so much when May was already caving and telling you everything you wanted to know. That's why you forced *him* to torture me. It was never about me... You've been going after him this whole time."

The general's face morphed into stern, harsh lines as bitter anger and resentment took their turns lighting the fire in his eyes. "Mr. de la Puente is a traitor to his country, as was his mother. But Raúl refuses to see the truth in front of him. He allows blood to cloud his judgment," he said, his pitch slowly rising. "And he ignores the warning of those who seek to serve him *best*!"

Shit...this was an old feud. Raúl, the general, and Javier's mother had history, no doubt about it. That history was still playing its wicked tune in the present, and it was going to cost us our *lives*.

The general shook, his whole body seeming to tremble with rage. "But it ends here—*today*," he declared. "And you're going to help me put to rest something that should have ended over a decade ago."

Holy stars, where was this going?

The general stepped to the small table, grabbed the cloth covering it, and lifted it away in one swift swoop. There, catching the light, were both my blades.

"Honor and Glory," I muttered under my breath.

"I can't say how delighted I was when I found both these items on his person," Harris explained. "You see, not only did Officer de la Puente fail to follow procedure when requesting serums above his pay grade, but he was in the position of contraband today. Imagine that," he added with a chuckle.

I looked at Javier, seeing his eyes burn bright. He kept them. He kept my blades the night I almost killed him. Harris's evil laugh made my skin crawl and my blood boil with rage. I turned my attention back to him.

"They're yours, aren't they? The ones you were supposed to use to kill him?"

I gritted my teeth, refusing to answer this asshole.

Harris waved me off. "Don't think that your silly refusals to answer my questions make any difference, my dear. Mrs. Huang told me everything I could want to know before she died in my chair."

My heart stuttered, backfiring in its cage. I resisted the urge to clutch my chest as the sharp pain stole my breath.

"Your mission was to kill him, yes? To assassinate the president's nephew as retaliation for my rather brutish tactics." He tipped his head back and laughed, his voice booming and echoing in the room.

My whole body began shivering as adrenaline pumped through my veins.

"Here's what I have to offer, my dear." The general rubbed his hands together once again. "I could really care less about you. No offense, of course. You've been a rather admirable foe, but my qualms rest with Officer de la Puente. You see, his mother was quite the upstart, and truly caused unnecessary problems from me. Her son has really followed in his mother's footsteps, and truly," he pinched his face, tipping his chin, "I'd really like to see him dead. It would bring me such joy," he added, looking like a saint, "so much, in fact, that I'm willing to make a deal."

My whole body froze, tingling with anticipation. Where was he going with this? What the hell was he going to do?

The general placed his hands behind his back once more, standing tall as his eyes narrowed into menacing slits. "I'm willing to offer you your freedom, Miss Le. And not just freedom, but the opportunity to reclaim your honor."

Thump, thump. Thump...ka-thump. Thump...thump.

Pain zinged through my solar plexus as every irregular beat caused my chest to tighten further. "What do you want from me?"

He smiled, and it was a smile that I swore would haunt me for the rest of my life if I lived to see another day. "To fulfill your duty, Miss Le. Fulfill your oath to your silly rebel alliance...take your knife and stab Javier de la Puente in the heart. Kill him, and I will let you free."

"What?" Tim shouted in a shocked growl at my side. But his father ignored him and just kept going.

"You could go home to your family, see their faces once more. Go home knowing that you fulfilled your duty to your faction, that you completed your mission," he added passionately.

I shook my head, taking a step back, only to feel Tim's gun pressing at my temple once more. "You wouldn't let me walk away that easily..."

General Harris looked wild—crazed. "Oh yes, I would, my dear. I don't think you understand the depths of my desire to see that boy die," he bit out through clenched teeth.

It didn't make any sense. "If you want Javier dead, then why don't you do it yourself? Why me?"

"That's none of your concern. I have my reasons that serve me well. All you need to know is that I am a man of my word." He pointed at Javi. "Kill him, and you go free."

"No." I shook my head. "I would never—"

"Do it," Harris snapped out. "Slaughter him like you were ordered to."

"You can't make me," I spat back.

The general scowled, his face going red. "You have a sister, correct? One that Mrs. Huang shared you love dearly…"

My jaw slackened. *No. Oh freaking stars, please no…*

"Do as I ask, Miss Le, and you'll see her again. Fail, and you will die. You've already been pronounced dead, remember? We place your body back in that bag and incinerate you, never to be seen or heard of again. But your sister," he said, lifting a pointed finger into the air, "Edith, isn't it?" Then his face twisted into a menacing scowl. His brows dipped into an exaggerated V, making his entire face contort into the most evil look I had ever seen. "I will personally hunt her down. I will find her and make her suffer in that fucking chair more than you ever did!"

"No!" I shouted, unable to contain the fear pooling in my gut as the image of Edith writhing and convulsing invaded my mind.

"Yes!" he screamed, his spit spraying the air. "You want her spared? Then kill Javier de la Puente and kill him *now*!"

Tears flooded my vision as I clamped my eyelids closed. I tucked my chin to my chest as my whole body trembled. *This can't be happening. I can't do this. It can't possibly come to freaking* this*!*

And just like before, time froze. Everything came to a dead stop. I lifted my face and watched as Edith materialized from the shadows of the room. Her long raven hair fell like silk over her shoulder as she stepped toward me.

Edith…you're back, I whispered.

She smiled, her dark brown boots stepping lightly, making zero sound as she passed the general. *I never left you, Lin.*

A tear rolled down my cheek. *It's all gone to hell, little sis, and I don't know what to do.*

Edith stood before me, a soft glint in her brown eyes. *Yes, you do. You know exactly what to do.* She took my hands in hers.

I blinked, feeling more tears fall down my cheeks as I shook my head. *I can't—*

You must, she insisted.

But I'm scared, I said, looking at our joined hands, squeezing them. How could they feel so devastatingly real? I looked back up at her. *What if I fail?*

The playful glimmer I always knew to be in my sister's eyes shimmered brightly. *Failing isn't the scary part. Never learning to fly is.*

My heart stuttered again, drumming its painful irregular beat.

Clasping our hands, she stepped closer, drawing them higher between us. *Fly, Lin,* she urged as her eyes bore into mine. *Let it fly.*

"Well, Miss Le, what will it be?"

I blinked, and Edith was gone. Harris took a step further, eyes still blazing like a wild man.

"Hágalo." I faced Javier, catching his eyes filled with so much passion, so much emotion. "Do it," he translated. "You don't have to choose; I'm making the choice for you. Do it. See your family. Hágalo, mi vida. No tengo miedo…I'm not afraid."

"How pathetically sweet," Harris said, his voice dripping in disgust. "I suppose your mother would have been proud of you, de la Puente. She seemed to turn your father into a pathetic sap."

Javier glared. "Vete a la chingada," he sneered at Harris. "Go to *fucking* hell."

"I'm going to love watching you die," he uttered through gritted teeth. The general whirled on me again. "How does this story end, Miss Le? Make your choice."

Thump…thump…ka-thump.

I looked at Javi once more as a single tear rolled down my cheek. "I'm sorry," I whispered to him.

His eyes flickered, lips pressed together, and then he nodded, accepting his fate. "Rápido, mi vida. Do it quick…right in the heart."

30: Level 20

I took steps toward the table just as General Harris put distance between us while Tim kept his gun trained on me the whole time. My knives sat quietly on the wood grain of the table, and I examined each one. Each steel blade glinted as the light from the room reflected back at me; their black hilts sturdy and worn, just as I remembered them.

Honor and Glory.

But they would bring me neither today. Today, they would bring me only death.

My hand stretched over the table, and I settled for Honor, curling my fingers over her black handle. Slowly, I turned and faced Javier.

"Very good, Miss Le, now onto the finale. Let's finish this."

I shot General Harris a piercing glare. *I will make him pay for making me do this.* I returned my attention to the duty at hand and stepped forward. Javier tipped his head back as much as the collar would let him, eyes steady on me as I took each step. And what killed me more than anything was that there was no anger, no hate, no hurt or regret.

All I saw was love.

Javier was nothing but love. He had always ever been *love*. There wasn't a bad cell in this man's body, and the Dissenters wanted to kill him simply because Raúl's blood pumped through his veins.

Fools. They were no fucking better than the Telvians, making the same shitty decisions that they did. Even if I were to make it out of here alive, I couldn't go back to them. I couldn't go back and continue to assassinate people who didn't deserve it simply because of blind allegiance. I had to change. It all had to change. There had to be a better way...

I stepped onto the platform, a grimace taking over my lips as I came to stand right before Javier. Slowly, I lifted the blade, pointing the tip over his heart. His eyes burned, and I remembered every caress of his hands, every taste of lips, every beautiful, accented word from his mouth. "Te amo, mi vida," he whispered. "Y te espero en las estrellas."

I sniffed, feeling one final tear roll down my check. "English," I reminded him.

He smiled...and oh holy fucking stars his smile and that look of pure sacrificial love in his eyes *ruined* me. "It means, I love you, and I'll wait for you in the stars."

I inhaled deeply. *Thump...thump...thump...tha-thump...*

"Amor vincit omnia," I whispered to him, forcing a smile on my lips. "Love conquers all."

His eyes narrowed, only for a second, and then I struck, everything happening within seconds. I pulled my hand back, and in one powerful strike, I slashed at Javier...slicing the leather strap at his wrist before spinning around, flipping my knife so I gripped it by the tipped point, and then threw it across the room.

Let it fly.

Honor spun and struck true, landing squarely in Tim Harris's right eye.

He screamed, dropping his gun, and falling to his knees as blood gushed from his face. The general sacrificed precious seconds, staring at his son writhing in pain, and I seized them. I launched myself off the platform, and charged General Harris, hitting him like a runaway train and sending us both careening to the floor.

I scrambled, reaching for the gun at his hip, unsnapping the holster and pulling it out just as—

WHAM!

I went flying to the right, seeing stars. The gun flew from my hand and clattered across the stone floor.

Get up, get up, get up! I rolled onto my hands and feet, scrambling to stand as another hit caught me in the gut. I collided back to the ground, rolling onto my back as the general came at me again.

"You stupid, girl!" he screamed, letting his boot hit me in the ribs. I shrieked, grabbing at my sides. He reached down and dug his hands in my hair, pulling me up to my knees. "I'm going to enjoy this. I'm going to watch you *fry*."

"Fat chance, asshole." I pulled back my elbow and let fly the hardest punch I could muster…right into his groin.

He doubled over in a slew of profanities, letting my hair go. I rolled, snapping to my feet, and then twirled in a spinning hook kick, catching my heel right in Harris's jaw, sending him hurtling to the floor as blood sprayed the stone.

I landed gracefully in my fighting stance, ready to take him again as I realized the general had landed only a mere few inches away from his gun.

No! I raced forward to kick it away just as his right hand clasped around the grip. Harris spun, lying on his back, and set the barrel right on me, freezing me in place.

"Bitch!" he spat out, blood sputtering from his mouth. "I'm going to murder you!"

Just as he was about to pull the trigger, Glory's blade sung through the air and pierced through Harris's right wrist, all the way down to the hilt, and protruded out the other side. The gun clattered out of his hand as Harris screamed out.

I spun around, catching sight of Javier, standing at the wooden table, hand still outstretched before slowly falling to his side. A wicked glint took over his eyes as he stood tall and smirked.

"God, I freaking love you," I said.

"I know," he replied.

I turned back to Harris as he panted furiously. I stepped around him and grabbed his gun from the floor before scanning the room. Tim was huddled in the corner, whimpering. Javier came to stand by me and held out a hand. I gave him the gun.

Slowly, he aimed it at General Harris. "Get up, General. Time for a taste of your own medicine."

To the general's credit, he didn't whimper. He didn't argue, protest, or complain. He rose to his feet, head held high, holding his arm with Glory still pierced through him. When Javier ticked his head toward the chair, he knew exactly what he was supposed to do. Ever the proud man, he stepped onto the platform, cradling his stabbed wrist, and the blood that dribbled everywhere told me he wouldn't live. If I had to wager a guess, Glory had sliced right through his ulnar artery.

Harris sat in the chair, sitting tall. "You're a disgrace to your uncle's name, Javier. You've betrayed your country—your *family*—and for what? A *girl*," he accused, wrinkling his nose as though the very thought soured his mouth.

"Tie him up, Lin."

"Dad!" Tim shrieked from the corner.

Javier glanced at him, lines of untamed rage painting his handsome face. "Move one muscle from that corner, Tim, and I'll shoot you." Tim cowered, curling into a tighter ball with a whimper, still clutching at his eye as he bled on the floor.

The general scoffed, glaring at his son. "Pathetic," he muttered.

Javi returned his attention to General Harris before catching my gaze and tipping his chin toward the chair.

I knew exactly what to do.

In moments, I had Harris, Sr. strapped down, improvising with the cut restraint on the one side. When I got to the other—the arm with Glory—I retrieved my knife, eliciting a hiss from him. Then I strapped that arm down too. If there was one man who deserved this, it was General Harris. How many lives had died in this chair because of him? It was only fitting he received the same justice.

Once Harris was secured, we both backed away from the platform, and I went to the computer, staring at the screen.

Javier stood just behind the caution line on the ground. "General Harris, I accuse you of murdering my mother—Serena de la Cruz. Do you deny it?"

My eyes widened as I looked at Javier.

Harris laughed. The asshole actually laughed out bitterly as blood splattered his front. "She was a traitor to Telvia," he admitted. "She would have seen this entire country fall with her ideals. I did what your uncle couldn't. I killed her, and I'd do it again."

Javier's chest rose deeply as he slowly faced me. "Max power, mi vida."

I blinked, trying to wipe the shock from my face as I returned my attention to the screen. With a few simple taps, the machine was ready—level 20.

"Que dios te perdone," he said to Harris. "May god forgive you, because I don't." Javier waved his hand. I swallowed hard and pushed the green button.

The machine whirred to life, and the very air vibrated with charged electrical energy as Harris screamed out, meeting his fate.

31: The Sunset

The power from the machine caused bolts of electricity to fly, and the entire room seemed to quake as General Harris's screams echoed relentlessly.

"It's going to blow, you stupid idiots," Tim cried from the corner. "It's too much power!"

"Time to go," Javier said, racing for me and taking my hands. Then we were running as bolts shot out from the machine, striking the computer, and then the table, and then...*everything*.

Javier threw open the door and ran out into the hallway as I caught one last look at the machine. Alarms blared, and red lights flashed in warning.

"Run, Lin!" I tore my attention away, following him down the hall. All the lights flickered, and I swore I could hear the electrical charge zinging through the bundles of cables above us.

WHOOP! WHOOP! WHOOP!

"What is that?" I screamed at him as we made another turn, and he busted through another door. It was a stairwell...an emergency stairwell.

"The power from the machine is wreaking havoc on the system. It's triggering everything to go off. *Climb!*" he ordered, taking the steps two at a time. Green, red, and blue lights flashed in the stairwell.

We rose several flights, passing several doors before Javier stopped in front of a door with a "0" painted on it. My eyes landed on a black key fob next to the door. "Do you have a way to open it?"

He hesitated.

BOOM!

The entire room quaked, and I stumbled on the stairs, my knees cracking on the concrete as I hit the ground. The stairwell lights flickered and went out, throwing us into darkness.

"Lin!"

"I'm okay. What just happened?" I heard several clicks, and then shuffling, and suddenly, light blinded me. I blinked rapidly until my eyes adjusted. Javier was in the doorway, and sunlight poured into the stairwell.

He grinned. "Looks like that electrical surge threw the power." I got to my feet, sending a silent *thank you* up to the heavens, and raced out the door. The heat of the sun on my face felt like a luxury I thought I would never feel again. I looked around and saw the large stretch before us. Parked military vehicles were ready for duty.

Javier grabbed my hand, pulled me forward, and then shoved me hard to the floor. My jaw dropped in surprise as I looked up at him and down the barrel of his gun…aimed right between my eyes.

"Javi?"

His name barely left my lips before someone shouted, "de la Puente!"

Suddenly, I understood. I didn't dare face the voice as I raised my hands up in surrender.

Javier's marred, beautiful face was nothing but a twisted scowl. "Sergeant."

A man, along with several REG officers, came into my field of vision. "What the hell happened to you, and what the fuck is going on with her?" the man ordered, pointing at me on the ground.

Javier never took his eyes off of me. "Prisoner transfer, sir. I just came from below," he offered as an explanation. "But General Harris…something happened while he was interrogating someone. The whole thing just blew up, sir. And this one almost escaped on me in the process," he said, motioning to the bruising and blood on his face with his free hand. "Violent thing, this one is," he added with a crooked grin as mischief lit up his eyes, still staring down at me. It took everything within me not to smile at the gentle nod to our shared past at the Academy.

"Shit," the officer muttered. "The fucking power surge blew every lock in the damn place. Opened every fucking cell door and now every inmate's loose. It's a freaking disaster. I've got officers radioing in riots down below."

"Did you call REG Command for help?" Javier asked, the gun still pointed at my face.

"Already done." The man looked down at me, then up at Javi. "I didn't hear anything about a transfer."

And suddenly, I felt cold. My gaze shifted between Javier and the sergeant before seeing Javier's free hand pat his chest, slipping into his uniform and pulling out a folded piece of paper. And just as before, when he spoke to the man, he handed the paper over without his gaze ever leaving mine.

"Orders from REG Command, sir."

What in the—?

The sergeant snagged the paper, looked it over, and then folded it back up before offering it back to Javi. "Fine. Take care of this one. But when you return, get your riot gear on and meet us below. We've got to contain this mess, and I'm ordering every officer to report down into the cell blocks until support from Command gets here."

"Yes, sir," he replied as he slowly tucked the paper back into the folds of his uniform.

"The rest of you, let's go!" the officer ordered. Flicking on his flashlight, the man waved and proceeded into the emergency stairwell, being followed by at least a dozen officers.

When the last one went through, Javier looked at me with a deliciously cocky grin as he lowered the gun.

"You want to tell me what the hell just happened?"

"Plan B," he said, and then he offered me a hand. "Vamonos, mi vida. Time to go."

Gladly taking his hand, I allowed him to pull me up even though I didn't need the help. "And what was Plan B?" I felt nothing but the exhilarating rush of adrenaline and pure love in my damaged heart as we walked on to find a ride.

"Let's just say having a cousin in REG Command has its perks."

My jaw hit the damn floor. "Cousin? As in *Jacob* de la Puente?"

He smiled as he looked over his shoulder at me, that mischievous gleam never leaving his black eyes. "Let's get outta here, mi vida." It was the only answer he gave me.

I shook my head, totally stupefied, because what just happened was another layer of evidence that there was more to Telvians than met the eye. They weren't all bad.

Mistaken, maybe.

But not necessarily bad. And it only confirmed for me what I had already decided. That Telvians could change, and there had to be another way to achieve the Dissenter revolution. Another option. Because Telvians didn't deserve to die…not without being given the chance to choose something different. To be given the opportunity to be better versions of themselves.

I followed Javier as he raced to the vehicle he already had prepared for us, and it was all over after that. Apex Rehabilitation Institute echoed with booms and gunfire as we saddled up and happily drove out the front gates before reinforcements from Telvia could arrive. And as I turned east, heading to the spot where I knew everything I needed would be waiting for me under a Joshua tree, Javier took my right hand in his and brought it to his lips.

"¿Qué hacemos ahora, mi vida? What now?"

I glanced at him before looking in the rearview mirror of the Humvee, seeing the camp as nothing more than a speck disappearing in the sunset behind me. I slipped my fingers from his, dragging them down the back of his hand to his wrist. Gently, I rotated it and ran my fingers over the single lotus flower. "We're going to find out what that symbol means… But first, we're going to find some cheeseburgers."

He tipped his head back and laughed, and the sound was deep and sinful and made my entire body tremble for him. "They better be orgasmic, mi vida, or I'm going to be disappointed."

I smirked as I faced the desert before us, now gripping the steering wheel with both hands. "Oh they *will* be, don't you worry."

"Te amo, Liddy Le."

"I know," I said, giving him a quick smile. "I love you, too."

Bonus Chapter: Javier

"Es demasiado inteligente para estar en Distrito Tres." The way she looked at me, I think she would have hit me if she could, and I respected her for that. Respected her ability to not be swayed by my title. Every other girl seemed desperate for me to look at them.

To speak to them.

To acknowledge their existence.

It was a constant problem Jacob and I both shared—to never know if someone liked you for who you were, or simply because of the power you wielded. Simply because of the title you carried.

But that wasn't the case with June.

She hated me.

No matter how many times I tried to impress her, to sweet-talk her, to do anything and everything that turned every other girl into a blubbering mess of batting lashes...

Nothing worked.

Everything I did received nothing but condemnation from her.

The way her body moved...

The way she glared...

The way she said my name like it repulsed her...

She absolutely *hated* me.

And though she bit her tongue most times, I knew she would revile everything about me if given the chance.

And I found that enticing.

"Whatcha say, man? Whatcha say?" Tim Harris looked at me—a grin plastered on his face. "Please tell me you called her Subclass Trash?"

I tried to suppress a sneer. Tim Harris could be such an ass, and the fact that he would even call her something so vile made me clench my jaw. I thought June was gorgeous—soft and strong, feminine but incredibly independent. I said that she was far too beautiful to be placed in District 3. I would never call her—or anyone for that matter—Subclass Trash, and the fact that Tim *would* turned my blood to acid. My mother taught me far better than that. But I had to hold back my temper with him—Tío Raúl's orders.

You need to get along with Tim, Javi. His father is important to the country. Don't disappoint me.

June whipped her head around to face me, and the moment I saw the soft supple lines of her face, I had to pull back the urge to stand up from my desk, march right up to her, and take her into my arms.

To touch her.

To savor the flavor of her mouth.

I tucked my chin, glancing at her under hooded eyes.

"Something like that," I lied, never taking my gaze off her.

"Speak *English*," she snapped at me. "At least have the guts to insult me in a language I understand."

Damn, I loved how she challenged me. Loved that she was something just out of reach, something that wouldn't fall so easily into my lap. Perhaps I was a glutton for torture, but everything about June fascinated me.

I leaned forward over my desk, arching a brow. "Acculturate yourself, mi vida. Then see if you have the courage to face me."

There it was…that look of pure hate. I could almost see the desperation in her to fight me. To scourge me with insults, pushing me to work harder. To be better.

And fuck, did I love it. Because the day I won June over would be the day I knew I had found a partner I wanted to spend the rest of my life with.

Watkins clapped her hands, bringing the attention back to her. "Enough, Mr. de la Puente. And please, speak in English."

I tipped my head at Watkins, but I couldn't take my eyes off June. Even as she turned her attention back to the professor, I was wonderfully ensnared at the sound of her voice. My thoughts drifted to graduation, to the thing I wanted more than anything…to be matched to June Huang.

I didn't care if we weren't in the same caste, I was going to try anyway. And if the Telvian Council refused our pairing, I'd have to do something to convince my uncle to allow it. Even if it meant sacrificing my one chance at autonomy in exchange for an opportunity to date June. I'd made it my life goal, as silly as it sounded to my cousin. Jacob knew how bad I had it for her—made fun of me for it even.

"You're seriously telling me your hope is to win June's heart?" He laughed at me once when we were home at the Presidential Palace. "No offense, Javi, but I think you could set greater goals for yourself."

"¿Y por qué, primo? Why?" I challenged him, translating. "As far as I'm concerned, there is no greater goal than to find your match, cuz. Your *soulmate*."

"Javi, the girl *hates* you. Even if my dad lets you match with her, there's no freaking way you'll ever win June's heart. She's got that shit locked up so tight, you'll spend a lifetime trying to find the key."

I chuckled. "Challenge accepted, primo. If my life is what it takes, then so be it. June will be mi vida, then. My life. I'm willing to sacrifice that." My eyes drifted to the tattoo on my wrist, reminding me of my mother. "Amor vincit omnia," I mumbled.

"What?"

I looked up at him. "Love conquers all, cousin. Call me a hopeless romantic to pursue June, but I have faith that one day, she'll see that I'm worthy of that heart she keeps tucked away."

Jacob shook his head, snickering in disbelief. "How about I call you *stupid* instead, huh?"

"Stupid is the man unwilling to fight for what he believes in. For abandoning a worthy cause simply because he fears failure."

"Whatever, Javi. I wish you luck."

I smirked at him. "I don't need luck, cousin. All I need is *faith*."

Thank you for reading *Revile*! I hope you enjoyed Liddy and Javier's story. If you enjoyed this book, please help an author out and leave a review on

Goodreads, Amazon, Barnes & Noble, or any other platform of your choice. As an indie author, the success of Liddy's story greatly depends on new readers finding it in a crowded marketplace. Your review helps new readers discover her, as well as me! It's the greatest gift you could give me. Thank you for considering writing a review.

Leave a Review on Amazon

Have you read the rest of *The Dissenter Saga* yet? Keep reading for release dates and book descriptions!

DISSENT
The Dissenter Saga, Book 1

The United States is gone. No one beyond the Wall can be trusted. And everything I knew was a lie.

In a world fractured by drought and ruled by tyranny, 17-year-old Mara de la Puente finds herself torn between loyalty, love and the fight for freedom. Accused of treason, she's thrust into the heart of rebellion, caught between two rebels vying for her heart: Matias, her guardian promising safety, and Wes, whose brooding gaze and turbulent past ignites a fire she can't ignore.

Navigating love and loyalty, Mara confronts her deepest fears amidst betrayal and intrigue, discovering her heart just might be the most dangerous battlefield of all.

For fans of *Shatter Me*, *Divergent*, and *The Hunger Games* world, *The Dissenter Saga* offers pulse-pounding action, jaw dropping twists, and heart-stopping dystopian romance. If you enjoy love triangles, enemies-to-lovers, "touch her and die" alpha males, action adventure, forbidden love, snarky humor, brooding anti-heroes, shocking plot twists, and a sweet romance that builds throughout the series, then *Dissent* is for you.

Are you ready to dissent?

Enjoy an exclusive sneak peek of *Dissent* after the Acknowledgments section!

Buy Dissent Now

RESIST

The Dissenter saga, Book 2

My brother sacrificed everything for me. I refuse to watch him burn. And I'll do anything to bring him home alive.

In a world of glittering gowns and conniving schemes, the survival of the rebellion teeters on the edge of a knife, and Mara de la Puente finds herself at the heart of a dangerous political game in a desperate attempt to save her brother's life.

But the safety of the North isn't as pure as it seems, and the path to salvation is treacherous, lined with deceit, betrayal, and unexpected alliances. As she navigates the deadly politics, Mara's heart is embattled with feelings for the sweet Matias Alvarez and a fiery passion for the brooding Wes Calvernon.

With time running out, her brother's life on the line, and the stakes higher than ever, Mara finds herself entangled in a web of deception and danger, where every decision could mean life or death for the ones she loves.

Resist is a gripping tale of love, sacrifice, and pulse-pounding action, where loyalty blurs with treason, and every jaw-dropping twist leaves you breathless. If you enjoy love triangles, snarky humor, arranged marriages, enemies-to-lovers, "touch her and die" alpha males, brooding anti-heroes, and a tantalizing slow burn romance that leaves you weak in the knees, then *The Dissenter Saga* is for you.

The rebellion must survive. Are you ready to resist?

Buy Resist Now

Coming January, 2025
RISE
The Dissenter Saga, Book 3

Love is always worth fighting for.

Subscribe to the Author Newsletter for updates on Rise!

Acknowledgements

Liddy's story began as a little spark: What would happen if a girl fell in love with her captor? Specifically, if that man was also her torturer?

Originally, her story was only supposed to be a novella—something I was going to offer for free to subscribers of my newsletter. But once I started crafting Liddy's tale and giving voice to her, I realized her story was so much bigger than just a little novella. And then, when initial beta readers fell in love with Javier and Lin's romance? Forget it! It was decided that *Revile* needed to be shared with the world.

I hope you enjoyed their story, and I hope you decide to read the rest of *The Dissenter Saga* if you haven't already. And don't worry (SPOLIER ALERT), you'll read more about Liddy and Javier in *Rise*.

I wanted to take a moment to thank all the people that made this story possible. To begin, thank you to my editor, Tayler Bailey McLendon from Bailey and Bloom Ink, who always gives 110 percent! Without her, there is a good chance you would have ended up with a "*they ran away and things were great*" type of ending. Yes, I am absolutely serious about that.

Next, I want to thank my beta readers: Ashley, Clara, and Melissa. They were hugely important in shaping this story. Their enthusiasm for Javier made me smile, and gave me the encouragement I needed to bring their romance to the world.

A huge thank you to my sister, Kassandra, is necessary. I knew I wanted Javier to be bilingual, and though I am a native Spanish speaker myself, I needed a second pair of eyes on the Spanish. Kassandra (who speaks Spanish beautifully) reviewed the Spanish to ensure that it was grammatically correct and that the translations into English were accurate.

Another shoutout to everyone who had to deal with my incessant pestering about book covers! Thank you, Clara, Kassandra, Karina, Gayleen, Liz, Tayler, Susan, Rachel, and Irianna, for helping me figure out the best cover for this story. I know I will forever be haunted by stupid lotus flowers.

Finally, thank you to my husband. If you can believe it, this man played a significant role in helping me tease out the finale for *Revile*. David, I hope you know how much I love you, and how important you are to every love story I write. Thank you for being my very own Rico Suave.

And finally, a *thank you* to you, the reader. You are the primary reason why I dedicate countless hours drafting, plotting, writing, and crafting story after story. At the end of the day, it is all for you, the reader. Thank you for taking this journey with me. I hope you will subscribe to my author newsletter and follow me on social media so we can discover new love stories together.

Subscribe to my Author Newsletter and get a downloadable *Revile* bookmark!

Subscribe to the Author Newsletter

And follow me on:

a amazon.com/stores/Josephine-Lamont/author/B0D1RKYZ6C

g goodreads.com/jlamontbooks

p pinterest.com/jlamontbooks

o instagram.com/jlamontbooks

f facebook.com/jlamontbooks

The United States is gone.
No one beyond the Wall can be trusted.
And everything I knew is a lie.

DISSENT

Copyright © 2024 by Josephine Lamont

0: Don't Fail

"Her Citizen ID is 1311?" He rubbed his goatee, brows sliding together as he considered the situation at hand.

"Yes." It was only one word, but her firm tone and body language communicated everything she needed.

The older man sighed, clearing his throat before protesting. "Madam President, what you're asking us to do is placing an unnecessary risk on our forces."

"I'm well aware of that, but I ask it of you nonetheless," she pushed back. Her gray hair rested neatly on her head in a tight, braided bun. Despite her petite stature, she stood tall and regal as she commanded the room.

The man rubbed his goatee once again, pulling on the peppered strands, staring off at the floor as he breathed in heavily through his nose. "We've never attempted something like this before. Trying to get into the Administration building is going to require intel we just don't have access to yet."

"Well then, get the access you need."

A second man, blond, with chiseled cheekbones and green eyes like meadow grass, chimed in, "It's impossible. The REG has tons of firewalls to protect access to the tracking chips. To hack into their system and deactivate her chip is, well…there's a reason why we've never done it before."

The woman closed her eyes, lips set in a thin line. Silence. Time ticked. Opening her eyes once again, she set her narrowed gaze on her subordinates, crows feet framing her eyes. "This rebellion depends on us outsmarting Raúl and his REG officers. And to do that, we must be willing to take risks to gain something greater. Removing her from the equation takes away his ability to hold her against us—"

"To hold her against *us* or to hold her against *you?*" It was a challenge. One that the woman met with a beady glare, causing the younger man to clear his throat. "I'm sorry, ma'am. I just can't help but be concerned—"

"Rest assured, gentlemen," she interrupted, her voice firm, cutting the man off like a knife. Her patience was wearing thin. "Whatever my personal attachments might be to the Telvian president or his child, I will always maintain what is best for our cause as my compass."

She stared both men down, her senior years carrying the full weight of her decades of experience and political leadership. "This rebellion must survive, and we must take Telvia back. We cannot tolerate the mistreatment of the people any longer." Her voice grew firm, *sharp.* "Raúl will lose this time. I will take myself to the grave before I allow him to continue to rule the regions. But to do that, we need more help. And to gain more help, I need *her.*" She paused for a moment, setting her gaze back on the blond man. "Can you do it? Or do I need to find someone else?"

Tension saturated the room. Both men looked at one another, nerves settling through their bodies as they shifted their weight from one foot to the other. Finally, the blond cleared his throat before speaking. "Yeah, I can do it. Consider it done."

The woman gave one firm nod. "Then get to it. Contact the others. We need everyone on this."

"Madam President, what if it doesn't work? What if we risk our moles just to fail? We'd have to start all over, and it took us *years* to get these people into position in Telvia."

She blinked, lifting her chin as her shoulders rolled back. "Then don't fail."

Both men glanced at one another before facing her once more. "Yes, ma'am."

1: Do It

"I was worried about you." Chase's voice was soothing, calm. How he always kept such control over himself, I would never know.

I looked up at the passing clouds of spring—white tufts of cotton, floating freely across the sky. Nothing told them what to do except the soft April breeze that whispered rain but brought none. The clouds had not a single care in the world.

Must be nice, I thought bitterly.

"Mara?"

"What? Oh! Yeah, I know. I'm sorry. You know I can't do anything when I'm in there."

Chase rolled onto his side, propping his head up with his hand. "Want to talk about it?"

I gave him a quick glance. *Did* I want to talk about it? I wasn't convinced it ever helped. Talking about it just made the memories more vivid, and I usually ended up crying like an idiot. And I *hated* crying in front of him. He was this beautiful, blond Adonis—refined cheekbones, a firm jaw, and light green eyes. Completely gorgeous. The last thing I wanted was to look ridiculous in front of him.

I shook my head, brushing back a swath of my brown hair from my face. I definitely didn't want to talk about it.

He opened his mouth, but hesitated. "Did…did she hurt you this time?"

I pressed my lips together as the memory resurfaced—my stepmom gripping me by the arm tightly as she dug her nails into my flesh, throwing me down the basement stairs. And then…the lashings.

The sensation of leather cutting into flesh...

The snap cracking in the air...

The feeling of warm, thick fluid dripping down my back...

My pulse quickened at the memory, and I instinctively reached for the golden heart pendant hanging around my neck. It was the first and last gift my father ever gave me when I was five—a small comfort in my dark world.

I didn't want to talk about what happened in the basement. I didn't want him to know. I didn't want *anyone* to know what it was really like. And the truth was, no one could know. Not ever.

"No." I glimpsed at him, hoping he'd drop it.

His eyes caught mine, and the gentleness of them sent a tingling buzz through me, sweeping out the fear. A smile curled onto his lips as he drew a hand up to mine, steadying my fingers on my pendant.

"You know, you don't have to lie to me."

My heart melted. Chase was the best thing that ever happened to me. I worked so hard to keep him away, denying him every time he came around offering to walk me home. But he was persistent, charming, and let's not forget, incredibly breathtaking to look at. It was no secret that Chase Beckham was the hottest thing around, and every girl at the academy practically dropped their skirts when he walked by. But, for some bizarre reason, he had chosen me. Of course, I shouldn't have been *that* surprised given that I was the First Daughter of Telvia. But I held no power, no amazing destined future. All *that* belonged to my older brother, Jacob.

"I just don't want to talk about it, okay? Can we drop it?"

His eyes searched mine, pleading, but I held firm. After a moment, he nodded. I gave him a quick smile before turning toward his chest and nestling into him, enjoying the warmth of his body against mine. We laid quietly for a few minutes, enjoying the heat of the sun and the sounds of the birds in the park. Feeling him stir, I looked up to see his face lost in thought. Curiosity got me.

"What are you thinking about?" I asked.

"You."

"Me?" Well, that was unexpected. "What about me?"

"Your birthday's next month."

I closed my eyes and buried my face in his chest. "I know."

He laughed, nudging me away from him. "Why do you say it like that? You're going to be initiated, and then you'll finally get to leave."

I flopped onto my back again, eyes staring up at the sky through the canopy of the fake spruce trees we rested under. The entire park was a fake. Nothing but artificial turf and plastic plants to create the illusion of a luscious garden. All of Telvia was like that.

"That's what *you* think," I countered. "That's what happens to people like *you*. But I'm not stupid…I know better."

He laughed again. *Great.* I'm glad he found my misery so amusing. "*People like me?* Now what's that supposed to mean?"

"When you turned eighteen, you got to be independent and move out. When *I* turn eighteen, I'm still going to be a slave to whatever my dad wants."

His eyes hardened. "He can't keep you in that house forever, Mara. You'll be eighteen, end of story. He'll have to let you go."

I snorted, "Yeah, *right*…" I drawled. "We'll see how that turns out for me."

Chase sat up then. "It doesn't matter if he's the president, you know." His brows pinched together in frustration. "The law says that when you're eighteen, you're assigned your new position and allowed to move on."

I covered my face with my hands because I could feel it—the lump forming in my throat and the tightness in my chest. I was on the brink. Chase wasn't wrong. That's the way Initiation was *supposed* to work. You submitted your application to the Telvian Administration, and it would get assessed by the Council. They scrutinized everything about you—your strengths, weaknesses, parentage, class—*all* of it. After that, depending how you measured up, they assigned you to your new, *permanent* life. The Council decided everything for you, from what district you would live in, to the job you would have, what class you would be in, and, eventually, who you could marry. It didn't matter what you wanted—no choices, no disagreements, no arguing, no discussion. End of story.

But I wasn't stupid.

I knew that leaving the Presidential Palace would never happen. When Jacob turned eighteen and initiated, he didn't get to leave either. Council just assigned him to a position at the REG—Rebel Enforcement Group—and ordered him to continue living at the palace. Why would I be any different?

On the one hand, maybe my parents would be happy to get rid of me. I wasn't even close to being the favorite, and I was pretty sure both my parents wished I had never showed up on their doorstep. But I had also been my stepmom's punching bag from the first day I arrived. I doubt she was going to allow me to leave when she gained such satisfaction from abusing me for everything I did. Belinda was my own personal devil.

I felt Chase's hands on my wrists as he pulled them away from my face. My vision blurred, and tears fell from my eyes when I blinked.

"Mara, they can't keep you there forever."

I sniffed, holding my breath, desperately trying to keep my emotions at bay. "You don't know how they are."

His eyes flickered with fervor. "You deserve better than living in that house."

That did it.

My whole life, my parents worked to make me feel like scum. To hear Chase say I *deserved* better caused my heart to ache. My chest tightened again, and the lump in my throat grew as another few tears rolled down my face. "Please don't... I don't want to talk about this anymore."

He grimaced, drawing a hand up to wipe my tears away. "You know, you're beautiful."

I sniffed again, but smiled as my cheeks reddened. "Stop. You're just trying to make me feel better."

He leaned down toward me, bumping his nose gently against my own. "Yes, *and* it's the truth." He placed a delicate kiss on my cheekbone, then another on my jawline, and a third at the corner of my lips.

Heat flourished within me as my chest swelled with breath. We were still new to each other. It had taken him months of pushing before I dared to let him in, thinking that I would just keep him at arm's length. But I quickly discovered that Chase had no intention of staying that far away from me. Each day, he grew bolder, more determined, more...*handsy*. And in the beginning, I slapped him, but he didn't give up easily. Now, here I was, practically aching for him to kiss me, to touch me *everywhere*.

I tipped my face toward him, giving him the perfect opportunity, mentally begging him to take it. Under hooded eyes, he looked into mine before casting his gaze downward toward my lips. My heart thundered in its cage. I knew this was wrong. I knew it was prohibited to get involved with someone without the Council's approval—without *Raúl's* approval. But I had never experienced such a deep want and desire inside of myself before. And I desperately wanted to feel *wanted*.

Chase's eyes swept back up to mine before gazing down at my lips once again. I could see his hesitation, his own desires, and his better judgment warring within him.

Just do it… Kiss me.

And then he leaned in, coming closer. It took everything within me to keep from shifting toward him to close the gap. I closed my eyes, tipping my chin upward, preparing myself to receive my first kiss.

2: Dissent. Resist. Rise.

Chase lowered his lips to mine—the briefest brush. The excitement that welled up within me was something fierce. My hands drew upwards around his neck, pulling him down towards me. But as quickly as it began, it was over. He pulled back. It was never anything more than a graze.

Disappointment washed over me as I opened my eyes. I was hoping for so much more. At least, I assumed it would be more. "Chase? Is everything okay? Did I do something wrong?"

He looked at me, giving me a hesitant smile before glancing around the park. "We just have an audience, is all."

I sat up, scanning around, and instantly understood his meaning. Telvian cameras. Privacy in Telvia wasn't a thing, and one misstep could mean a lot of problems for a person.

"I don't want to upset Raúl. Besides, if I'm going to get permission to be a potential match for you, I want to keep myself in his good graces."

What? Did he seriously just say...?

My expression must have given me away, because Chase laughed before planting another kiss on my cheek. "I told you I liked you. I wouldn't have been so stubborn about getting you to like me if I wasn't attracted to you."

"I don't know," I teased. "Are you sure it's that you like *me*? Or is it that you like my title as the First Daughter of Telvia, hmm?"

He slapped his hand to his chest, covering his heart. "Ouch! How could you think so low of me?" he bantered back before scooping my hand into his. "Last time I checked, having Raúl inspect my record that closely is something most

Noble Class citizens would want to avoid. I, on the other hand, will risk it if it means I get a chance at getting to know you better."

Everything within me tingled at his intentions. At eighteen, I would be eligible to be courted, but all potential prospects would need to apply for permission from the Council. If the Council thought the match was appropriate, we could date. And that idea lit me up from the inside out.

My skin prickled with excitement. Maybe I *could* leave that house and start a new life. Get away from all the crap that was my reality. Maybe…maybe I could actually be happy.

"Come on, I'll walk you home." He lifted himself up and offered me a hand. I took it, a dorky smile plastered across my face as he pulled me up and against his firm chest, the space between us disappearing. His left hand circled around my back while his right laced our fingers together. I tipped my head upward, meeting his light green eyes as my cheeks flushed.

Then we both heard it.

A scream.

We both turned toward the cry coming from across the artificial grass and within the entanglement of concrete buildings.

"Stop it! Please!" Another yell rang out. It was clearly a child. I felt Chase let me go as he took off toward it, and I followed closely behind.

"Stand still, you little maggot!"

Another scream.

We crossed the lawn in seconds, running through the street and onto the sidewalk. Chase whipped around the corner of the first building and came to an abrupt halt. I nearly ran into him, but stopped in time, feeling the momentum push me forward onto my toes before I rocked back onto my heels.

Chase stood rigid like stone, solid and unwavering, his focus down the alley. About midway down stood a Telvian Enforcement Officer, dressed in his white and black plated armor, towering over a young boy crumpled on the ground. The boy stretched his hand out toward the officer.

"Stop it!"

"*Shut up*," the man sneered as he lifted his assault rifle into the air and then slammed the butt end down on the boy. The child screamed out again.

My whole body jumped at the sickening smack of the gun making contact with the lump of flesh, and I didn't think. My body reacted out of its own volition. I hustled around Chase and yelled, "Stop!"

The officer lifted his weapon again and then rammed it down once more. Before I knew what was happening, my hands were on him, yanking on his arms and pulling him away from the boy.

"I said, *stop!*"

The man whipped around, shoving me back while throwing his right arm across his chest. Right as he swung it back toward me in a back-handed assault, Chase dove in front of me, pushing me back with his left hand while holding out his right to block the blow.

But it never came.

The officer froze as he took us in, confused. I knew he'd never had someone step in like this before. Hell, *I* couldn't believe I had just done what I did. He gave a scathing glare at Chase before setting his eyes on me.

"How dare you interfere with Enforcement?" he growled through gritted teeth.

My heart pounded, threatening to break through my ribcage. Chase turned his body to stand directly in front of me, putting both his hands up in surrender. "Hey, we're not here to interfere. We heard screaming and thought someone needed help."

"No one needs you here, so *scram*. This is none of your concern."

I placed my hand over my heart, pushing against the violent beats, letting out a breath. "Please forgive us," I said. "I'm Mara de la Puente." Chase kept his stare firmly on the officer, but slowly lowered his arms. The man brought his rifle down in response, and I took it as a sign that the drama was over. Trying to settle my nerves, I took in deep, full breaths.

Stepping out from around Chase, I tried to gather my courage and spoke. "Tell me," I began, pulling myself up to my full height, which isn't much when you're only five foot five. "What happened here? What did this boy do to deserve this?" I chanced a glance at the child, and my heart seized. His lip was split open, one eye swollen shut, and I suspected the other eye wasn't far behind.

The officer rolled his shoulders back. "You're the president's daughter? I don't recognize you."

I gulped. "Yeah, I get that a lot, but I'm his daughter. My Citizen ID is 1311. You can perform a retinal scan if you need to."

He eyed me up and down and then shifted his gaze to Chase. He hesitated, calculating, and then he looked back at me. With narrowed eyes, he cleared his throat. "I think you'll agree, Miss de la Puente, that this little shit deserved what he got and more." He pointed at the alley wall, guiding my vision to a huge reelection campaign poster.

I recognized this one. It was the same one my father used in his past several elections, since the very beginning. The poster was life-sized, showing Raúl standing tall, decorated with his medals, looking straight at you. Behind him were trees, flowing water, laughing children and families.

Raúl de la Puente
A vote for Raúl is a vote for a sustainable future.

It was a good one. A gentle reminder that our very existence depended on water, a resource that the earth could give plentifully or just as easily take away. The Great Drought had been hard on us all, leaving only extreme choices as our options for survival. And when Raúl became president, he made those tough calls, carrying the weight for the rest of us. It meant extreme rationing of water and food and the development of a caste system. Those who were determined to be of high value to the preservation of humanity's future were placed in the Noble Class and given access to more of those needed resources. Those who were thought to be problematic, defective, or just coming from *bad stock*, were placed in the Subclass. The Administration still took care of them, but what they received was…well, not as much.

The poster was definitely a brilliant piece of propaganda, but that wasn't what the officer was pointing at. It was the giant, red graffiti painted across it.

Dissent
Resist
Rise

My jaw hit the floor. "Oh my god…" I covered my mouth with my hands. This wasn't good. This was bad…*really* bad.

Chase stepped forward, putting a hand on my shoulder. "The boy did this?"

"That's what I suspect. I came around the corner and noticed there was a Subclass citizen out of his district in the alleyway. I was planning on escorting him back into District 3 when I noticed this." The man tipped his head toward the defiled poster. "As you can see, miss, the boy clearly deserved what he got."

I looked at him and then at the boy, fear huge in his eyes. How would I get him out of this? I looked back at the poster, reading the words again. Raúl was going to be livid. There had been no one bold enough to engage in this kind of rebel activity. Not in the Noble Class District, anyway. Movement caught my eye, and I turned to watch Chase. He stepped up to the poster, eyeing it up and down before running a finger across the paint. Rubbing his fingers together, he turned to face me.

"It's dry."

"What?" I didn't get it. So what if it was dry?

Chase held up his finger so I could see it. *Clean.* "It's dry. If that kid did this, it wouldn't be dry already. There's no way it was him." He turned and faced the poster again. "This has been up here for at least an hour."

The officer shifted on his feet. "Rubbish! This little shit was here, and I caught him right-handed."

I looked back at the man. "You *saw* him paint this?"

His brows furrowed. "No, but the brat was here."

Chase turned back toward us. "Circumstantial evidence."

The sneer returned to the officer's face as he pointed down at the kid. "He's out of his district."

I gulped. He was right. The child shouldn't have been here. I faced the boy again as he laid crumpled on the floor. He couldn't have been over eight, maybe seven. The realization caused a memory to flood me. A memory of myself in a loose heap on the floor of a cold, damp basement.

Hungry…

In the dark…

Bloodied…

For days.

My heart ached. Though this boy was a member of the Subclass, in so many ways, I saw myself.

I took another deep breath. "Did you do this?"

The boy looked at me and vigorously shook his head.

I pointed at the poster. "You swear to me you didn't do this?"

"N-no. No, ma'am," he stuttered, eyes wide.

"Why are you in District 1?"

He looked at the officer, fear clear in his eyes.

"Don't worry about him, look at me. Why are you in District 1?" I felt for him, I really did. But I needed something—*anything*—to help me absolve him.

The child swung his gaze back to me. "I-I was looking in the trash for nourishment pills."

"Why?"

"We're starving in District 3."

"Lies," the officer spat out.

"Hey!" Chase warned, his voice deep and gruff. "The First Daughter of the Presidential Family is asking the boy a question." Chase emphasized my title, making sure it sunk in *real* deep with this man. "Show her your respect and allow the boy to answer her."

The officer glared, but he kept his mouth shut.

I returned my attention to the child. "Nothing in the trash would be useful to you."

"I'm sorry, miss." He looked away from me then. There was more. So much was being left unsaid, but I didn't want to sit around and dig for answers. I looked at Chase.

"If he did it, where are the paint cans?" Chase motioned around us, and my gaze followed him. He was right. There were no cans, brushes, or anything to be seen.

I nodded. "Officer, thank you for your diligent duty in maintaining peace and order. The boy has received enough punishment for being in the wrong district. I suggest you put in a work order immediately to have this mess cleaned up, and be sure you notify the REG as soon as possible about this rebel activity."

The man narrowed his eyes, piercing me with a look that screamed he was pissed. My stomach turned, making me feel sick, and just as I thought I was going to cave under his unforgiving gaze, he finally nodded in agreement.

"What about him?" he motioned toward the boy.

"We'll take care of the kid," Chase offered. I looked at him before returning my attention to the officer. The look he gave us was pure venom, and somewhere deep within me, fear trickled in. I knew this wasn't over. It was only just the beginning…and I was going to pay dearly for it.

3: WTF?

All I could do was stare at the words, reading them over and over again.

Dissent

Resist

Rise

I knew rebel activity had been growing in the Subclass district. There were even some rumors of it spreading to District 2…but *District 1*? Raúl was going to lose his mind, especially with Election Day only two months away.

"Do you think he did it?" I was pretty sure the boy was innocent, but another part of me was growing nervous. What if he *did* do it? What was going to happen to me if that man told my parents I intervened in an Enforcement officer's duties?

Chase came up to stand beside me. "No, I really don't." Silence filled the space, but only for a moment before he bumped my shoulder. "Letting him go home was the right thing to do. You made the right call."

I glanced at him before shifting my gaze back to the blaring red letters smeared across my father's face. "Did I?" I blew out a breath. "I hope you're right." Silence fell between us again as we both took in the vandalism. "Why would somebody do this?"

Chase snorted. "Isn't it obvious?"

"What?" I frowned.

Chase looked at me straight on. Nothing about him gave off any sense of hesitation. "What part of this is confusing to you? Telvia's growing restless, Mara. People aren't happy." He looked back at the poster, seriousness enveloping his angular features. His words came out low and deep, as though he had forgotten I was there and was thinking aloud. "Raúl's overstayed his welcome."

Something ignited within me. "Are you nuts? He's been voted in twice already. *Clearly*, the people love him."

Chase crossed his arms, eyes never wavering, "Could it be the election's a farce? No one's ever run against him, so of course he would win every time."

My jaw hit the floor. I couldn't believe I was hearing this from him. Yes, it was true no one ever ran against my father, but clearly no one thought they could do better, *right*? An inkling of doubt settled deep within me, and I hesitated.

No. Raúl was a good leader. Everything he did was to protect the Telvian people…*all* of them. I had to believe that. I was his daughter. Because if I didn't believe it…if I was wrong about him, then—

I couldn't finish the thought. That kind of thinking only led to trouble. And I had enough trouble plaguing me already.

Chase turned to face me, arms still folded across his chest. "It's only natural that when people feel oppressed, they rise up." He pointed at the ruined campaign poster. "I mean, look at this. This isn't District 3, Mara. Someone in the Noble Class did this."

I didn't want to hear it. My mind attached to one word, and that word kept zipping through my consciousness. "*Oppressed?* You know, it's not like shit's been easy for him. And *clearly* the Telvian people placed him in power because they believed he could guide us through the drought. That was some real crap, Chase, and you know it. And he did it. He got us through."

Chase looked up at the sky as he exhaled, exasperation setting in. "Yeah, he did, Mara, but he's been in power *too* long—"

"*What?* Are you insane?" I looked around, checking to make sure no one heard him. Grabbing him by the shirt, I shoved him deeper into the alley before whisper-yelling at him. "Are you crazy? How the hell are you even talking like that? Someone could hear you!"

His brows knitted together, tension growing thick between us. "Who cares who hears me?" It wasn't a question, but a challenge.

"*I* care! Last time I checked, you wanted my father's favor, *remember?*" That did it. Chase's eyes flickered, emotion passing through them before he blinked. When he opened them again, his expression softened as he cleared his throat.

"You're right. You're absolutely right." He looked over his shoulder before looking back at me. "I'm sorry. I'm—I just...I just want to make sure that stuff like this doesn't happen anymore, ya know? And figuring out why someone would defile your dad's poster is an important step in making sure that something like this doesn't happen again."

I guess that made sense...kind of. But it didn't help me feel any better or any less annoyed with him. I crossed my arms, giving him a dubious look.

He shifted his weight, inhaling deeply before speaking again. "I'm sorry, Mara. I...I don't know why I got all fired up. I shouldn't have said anything."

Part of me felt relieved, but something else told me this wasn't over. He must have noticed that I was unconvinced, because he gave me that smirk I loved so much. Two simple steps and the gap between us dissolved as he planted a simple kiss on my cheek.

"I've got to go," he said.

"Go?" I started, confusion mixing with my unease. "What do you mean *go*? Aren't you going to walk me home?"

"Yeah, um..." he stuttered, looking off into the distance. "I forgot I have something to do for work. You can get yourself home, though, right?"

"Uh, yeah. Yeah, I can get home from here," I replied. This was so not like him. I mean, WTF?

"Good." He walked backwards as he began to leave the alley. "I'll call you tomorrow." Then he turned and left me standing there...alone, feeling like, somehow, I was the one who did something wrong. Reaching for my little heart, a shiver flowed down my spine, and I suddenly felt cold in the shadows of the alley.

WANT TO FIND OUT WHAT HAPPENS NEXT?

ORDER YOUR COPY NOW

Follow Me on

instagram.com/jlamontbooks

goodreads.com/jlamontbooks

amazon.com/stores/Josephine-Lamont/author/B0D1RKYZ6C

pinterest.com/jlamontbooks

facebook.com/jlamontbooks

About the Author

Josephine Lamont is a Cuban-American author, living in Covina, California. She is a lover of all romantasy stories and enjoys writing tales of strong women facing impossible odds and sexy book boyfriends. When she's not hard at work writing, she spends her time reading, watching ghost documentaries, camping, or hanging out with her family. Josephine loves connecting with her readers. Visit her at jlamontbooks.com

Milton Keynes UK
Ingram Content Group UK Ltd.
UKHW040909191024
449793UK00010B/101/J